enchanting christmas

An Impossible Dream Novella

BETH CIOTTA

ISBN-13: 978-0692349045
ISBN-10: 0692349049

ALSO BY BETH CIOTTA

Impossible Dream

BEAUTY & THE BIKER
ENCHANTING CHRISTMAS
MARRY POPPINS

The Cupcake Lovers

FOOL FOR LOVE
THE TROUBLE WITH LOVE
ANYTHING BUT LOVE
SOME KIND OF WONDERFUL
IN THE MOOD FOR LOVE

A Wild West Romance
LASSO THE MOON
ROMANCING THE WEST
FALL OF ROME

The Glorious Victorious Darcys
HER SKY COWBOY
HIS BROKEN ANGEL
HIS CLOCKWORK CANARY

For an extensive booklist, visit Beth's website
www.bethciotta.com

PRAISE FOR BETH CIOTTA'S NOVELS

"Charming, witty and magical. A Must-Read!"—*Tasty Read Book Reviews* (on *Beauty & the Biker*)

"Filled with humor, heart and touch of mystery, this is a truly magical book." –*Born to Read Books* (on *Beauty & the Biker*)

"Deep love of family and strong dialogue bolster a refreshing romance that focuses on the emotional rather than the physical." –*Publishers Weekly* (on *In the Mood for Love*)

"Ciotta writes fun, sexy reads with a good dose of realism." —*RT BOOKreviews* (on *The Trouble With Love*)

"Ciotta's wit adds spark to this tale of extended-family joys and sorrows, smalltown living, and complicated characters." –*Publishers Weekly* (on *Fool for Love*)

"Enchanting contemporary romance." –*Publishers Weekly* (on *Charmed*)

"Ciotta has written another imaginative, whirlwind adventure, featuring a daring hero and a spirited heroine, incredible inventions, and übernefarious villains." —*Booklist*, starred review (on *His Clockwork Canary*)

DEDICATION

To the BC Dream Team...
My champions and fellow dreamers!

One

Once upon a November

Here's the thing about small towns. Especially small towns that are almost ghost towns. The people who've bothered to stick around go whole hog when it comes to making merry. Festivals, fairs, bicentennials, holidays. They adorn the storefronts—even the abandoned ones—drape banners from the traffic lights—singular in this case—hang decorations from the lampposts.

Even with Thanksgiving a full week away, Nowhere, Nebraska—population 1000 and dropping—was already decked out for Christmas. Chrissy didn't mind the visual aspect. But she did mind the assault on her ears and heart. Ringing from every speaker in every store, seasonal classics celebrating all things St. Nick and baby Jesus. Lyrics and melodies geared to inspire wonder, faith, and hope.

Chrissy had a beef with music in general, but songs of yuletide joy made her particularly twitchy. Just now a symphonic rendering of *Have Yourself a Merry Little Christmas* scraped over her soul like a rusty blade. Even though her friend's voice and the clatter of food being served overshadowed the wistful melody, Chrissy turned downright cranky. So much so that when Georgie finished sharing her exciting news, Chrissy responded with a churlish, "No can

1

do."

"You're kidding, right?"

"Do I look like I'm kidding?"

Georgie flicked her long, dark hair over her shoulders then angled her head and studied Chrissy with squinty emerald eyes. "You look like you just sucked on a whole bag of lemons. Not for anything, but for someone whose name is Christmas, you sure are a Scrooge."

Chrissy, who'd been born Christmas Joy Mooney twenty-eight years ago this coming December twenty-fifth, smirked at one of her oldest and dearest friends. "Bite me."

Undaunted, Georgie pressed on. "Come on. A weekend getaway! Holiday wonder in the Mile High City! A magical adventure for the Inseparables plus One! Even Sinjun is flying in."

The "plus One" being Chrissy's four-year-old daughter, Melody. The "Inseparables" meaning Chrissy, her cousin, Bella Mooney, and their longtime friends Georgina Poppins, Emma Sloan, Angel Drake, and Sinjun Ashe.

Sinjun was the only long-distance member of their BFF club and Chrissy, the youngest of the lot, was the only one who had a kid. None of them were married, although Bella was engaged and Angel was twice widowed. The six of them had been a close knit group ever since they were children. They'd made a pact, swearing friendship forever and a lifetime in Nowhere. Sinjun had fudged the second part but that wasn't her fault. She'd only been thirteen when her Mom announced they were moving to the east coast. It wasn't not like Sinjun could refuse.

"Listen," Georgie said. "The second weekend of December is the only weekend that works for everyone. Including you. I asked about your availability two weeks ago."

"But you didn't say anything about a trip to Denver." The mere mention of that city knotted her stomach.

"I was in the planning stages, and now I'm not. It's all set and it wasn't easy. You have to go. It won't be the same without you!"

"All right, all right. Calm down." An intensely private person, Chrissy glanced over her shoulder. "People are listening."

People being a handful of citizens who'd braved a bitter

cold night in order to enjoy the cozy ambiance and good food of Nowhere's historical Café Caboose. Historical because the main part of the eatery was a late nineteenth-century rail car, renovated and augmented with a long luncheon counter, spinning stools, and several cushy booths. The Inseparables had been meeting here every week for close to fifteen years. They were as much a fixture as the "Travel by Train" clock with the buzzing neon lights hanging above the front door.

Or at least they used to be. Tonight it was just Chrissy and Georgie.

"Sorry," Georgie grumbled under her breath. "It's just we see less and less of each other these days. This," she said indicating their table for two, "is a prime example. When's the last time three out of five of us bailed on our weekly dinner? I know everyone's busy. Hell, you're busy, but you made it. And I thought, 'Great! Okay! At least I can celebrate with you.' I worked my butt off coordinating a fabulous, affordable, magical getaway. I'm sorry I snapped, but a little enthusiasm would've been nice. Just saying."

Looking dejected, Georgie—who'd been suffering a crazy string of bad luck for months—turned her attention to the menu.

Feeling like a jerk, Chrissy slumped back against her upholstered seat and dissected her prickly mood. Yes, the music had lit her fuse, but she'd been on a slow burn for years. Amazing that her friends and family continued to love her because, honestly, most of the time there wasn't a whole lot to love. Resentment, anger, and self-disgust had turned her into a Grinch on wheels. She'd even abandoned her given name, Christmas, because it only reminded her of the spirited dreamer she'd once been.

Almost five years had come and gone since Mason Rivers, tabloid serial-dater, had tainted her life. She'd finally grown tired of her restless and bitter mindset and a few months back had vowed to adopt a more positive approach to life.

She'd braved a new haircut—a sassy, shaggy "do" that complimented her naturally straight, platinum locks. Launched *Gypsy Folk Yarns*, an on-line knitted goods store that offered her unique designs—scarves, cowls, ponchos, caps, and gloves, to name a few. Between her new knitting endeavor and her longtime job at Buzz-Bee's Bakery, finances were finally looking up. She'd even gone on a couple of dates although those hadn't been nearly as satisfying or successful as her new cyber business.

She wasn't sure anyone understood how difficult it was for her to break free of the week-long affair that had changed her life. Naïveté and poor judgment had led to a shattered dream and broken heart. Certainly no one knew the depth of her anxiety regarding the welfare and happiness of her sweet daughter. Like most of the Mooneys, Chrissy internalized her ugliest battles.

"I'm sorry," she said to Georgie after the waitress took their orders. "I didn't mean to be a buzz kill. Tell me more about your plans."

"Seriously?"

"I'm all ears." *Even though my interest is half-hearted.*

Georgie, who was famous for shrugging off rejection, lit up like a freaking Christmas tree. "I know finances are tight," she said. "I'm barely getting by myself. Trust me, this getaway is ridiculously affordable. We can car pool to Denver in four hours and you won't believe the rate I got on a two bedroom suite. Also, think of the money you can save on last minute Christmas presents by shopping at the outlets."

"There is that," Chrissy said, trying her best to get on board.

"Angel's been to Denver during holiday season. She swears Melody will think she's visiting the North Pole. The seasonal decorations are out of this world. The only thing I couldn't secure were seven tickets to the Mile High Christmas Extravaganza," Georgie said. "Already sold out. Can you believe it? But there are plenty of holiday displays and festivities including a parade!

"I don't mean to pressure you," she went on, "but we're all in need of a breather from this dying town and our intensifying challenges. Even Bella, who's disgustingly in love with Savage, expressed a desire to kick up her heels with the girls."

Chrissy felt her resolve slipping. She knew everyone needed a break from the pressures of their individual lives. Hell, she needed a short reprieve from the mounting stress regarding her and Melody's future. She hadn't discussed it with anyone other than her mom and dad, but she'd been wrestling with the advantages of moving to a larger town. Melody would start Kindergarten next year and, as a child who'd been born profoundly deaf, her learning options via local schools were limited. Chrissy wasn't thrilled about distancing herself from family and friends, but Melody's education was a massive consideration.

"It's just...I wish you would have picked another destination," Chrissy said while mindlessly fiddling with her knife.

"What's wrong with Denver? Yes, it's out-of-state, but it's a heck of a lot closer than Lincoln or Omaha."

Rather than turning in on herself, Chrissy sat straighter. A couple of months back, via an ultra-private video chat, Sinjun had mentioned how Chrissy's secrecy regarding the father of her child only gave the man more power over her life. Chrissy wasn't ready to reveal all, but she saw no advantage in another lie. Therefore, she stated her problem with Denver. "He-who-shall-not-be-named lives there."

Georgie gawked. "Benedict Romeo?"

Cheeks burning, Chrissy shushed her.

"The dirt bag who sicced a lawyer on you?" Georgie whispered. "The sack of—"

"Yeah. Him." Chrissy folded her arms over her churning middle.

"You told us he lived somewhere in state."

It was one of the few facts, albeit vague, that Chrissy had given up. "He did. Until recently."

"I thought you severed all ties after—"

"I did."

"But you're keeping tabs on him?"

"Not on purpose." Chrissy sighed knowing she had to give up something else otherwise her friend would press for a full account. "He was mentioned in the news a while back. Relocated to Denver on business."

She'd been researching state wide assistance and advancement for the deaf and hearing impaired—she did that a lot—when she'd tripped upon an article announcing the relocation of Mason Rivers, golden boy and heir of Rivers' Audio & Video Inc. Or RAVI as the company was now famously known. The fact that Mason and his family made millions revolutionizing and promoting audio equipment and concert venues while the daughter he'd forsaken lived in silence was just one of the reasons Chrissy resented the manipulative heartbreaker.

"He's a musician, right?" Georgie asked. "What? Did he get famous or something? How did he rate a mention in the news? When? Where? The newspaper? Television? Radio? Online? For God's sake, Chrissy. It's been five years. Give up the ghost."

She shook her head. "My dad and brother would kick his ass if they knew who he was."

"Can't say he wouldn't deserve it."

"Except he could retaliate." Mason's lawyer, or rather his mega-rich family's lawyer, had made that point loud and clear. "I can't risk it." Tamping down her growing frustration, Chrissy blew out a breath. "Listen, I don't want to talk about him and I don't want to risk running into him. Especially not with Melody along. Hence my problem with Denver."

"The on-going mystery regarding the identity of Benedict Romeo aside," Georgie said, "what are the chances of running into him in a city as big Denver? Although I guess any chance is bothersome. I'll cancel the trip."

Georgie was backing off, just like Chrissy hoped. Even so, she felt no joy in her friend's acquiescence. In fact, her mood worsened.

"We don't have to do a full-out holiday weekend," the resilient woman went on. "Maybe I can book us a cheap cabin closer to Nowhere. Who needs Christmas hoop-la? We can make our own magic. Also, not to spoil the surprise, although I am, we'd planned on celebrating your birthday that weekend. You always get shortchanged on celebrations considering you were born on Christmas day. Anyway, that's another reason why the trip wouldn't be the same without you."

Chrissy frowned. *Why do I feel like the most self-absorbed person on the planet?* No Inseparable's life was a bed of roses and yet no one else had a stick up their butt like she did.

"I may be a Scrooge," she said as the waitress showed with their food, "but I refuse to ruin everyone else's fun, not to mention my birthday surprise." She glanced at Georgie, feeling like a jerk because Georgie, although a bit of a screw-up, had a heart as big as Nebraska. "I know you worked hard to make all the arrangements. And Angel's right. Mel will love it. Sorry to be a pain. Count me in."

Georgie beamed then faltered. "What about risking a run-in with he-who-shall-not-be-named?"

Chrissy shrugged, pretending indifference and willing optimism. "Like you said, what are the chances?"

Two

Once upon a December

"What's with all the boxes? Don't tell me you haven't unpacked yet?"

"In that case, my lips are sealed." Mason Rivers stepped aside as the force-of-nature that was his mother blew past him and the half-dozen cartons stacked in the hallway. He offered to take her coat. She declined.

Good. It meant she wouldn't be staying long. Although, with Priscilla Rivers, five minutes could seem like a lifetime.

He heard her grumbling as she passed the kitchen, signifying her disgust at spying more boxes. At least every box was uniformed—important for a neat freak like Prissy— all the same size. All stamped with RAVI, the acronym for their family's company. There were more in his bedroom and several in the spare room that served as his office. Luckily, she headed straight into the living room.

"Can I get you anything?" he asked. "Coffee? Brandy?" *A sense of humor?*

"Just a towel. A *clean* towel."

"Right." Because he'd dare to offer his perfectionist mother a soiled one. Praying for patience, he slipped into the bathroom and raided the linen closet. While there, he stole a

8

look in the mirror. Hair in need of a comb and a trim, bloodshot eyes, a day's growth of beard. The look of a man battling insomnia or a severe hangover. In his case both. Amazing his mother hadn't mentioned his ragged looks although maybe she'd been too busy sizing up his digs to notice.

Annoyed by her unannounced visit, he moved back into the living room to find his obsessively stylish mother assessing his highly impersonal accommodations.

Even though he'd declared Denver his new stomping ground, his restless spirit said otherwise. Unwilling to invest time and thought into temporary lodging, he'd purposely rented a fully furnished apartment. That included window treatments, wall art, scattered sculptures, and kitchenware. He'd unpacked essentials only—clothes, electronics, favorite coffee mug, his battered, but beloved, guitar, and Rush's bedding and toys. The rest of his belongings—aka various crap collected throughout the years—remained in bubble wrap and cardboard.

He flicked his hand toward the organized chaos. "I'll get around to it."

"When? You moved into this condo three months ago. Don't tell me you're strapped for time. It's not like you punch a clock."

He hadn't punched a clock when he'd worked out of the main office either, but he had been under the family's thumb. As the sole surviving son and heir of RAVI, for the last five years his parents had ridden shotgun over his professional and personal life. Partly because they were control freaks. Mostly because they were afraid if, left to his own devices, Mason would end up meeting with the same fate as his older brother, James. Maybe not as grim, but dead is dead.

"What are you doing here, Mom?"

"I need a reason to visit my son?"

"No. But I'm not exactly around the corner." He passed her the towel, then folded his arms and leaned against the wall as she inspected his furniture, no doubt looking to perch in a Rush-free zone. Good luck with that.

"Why are you in Denver?" he tried again. His parents lived in an affluent suburb of Lincoln, Nebraska. Seven hour drive from their door to his. Under two hours by air.

Knowing his mom, she'd chartered a plane. The question was, why. "And don't tell me you flew in for an afternoon of Christmas shopping," he said, borrowing one of her favorite sentence starters.

After frowning at his sofa and scowling at the matching love seat, she spread the towel on the ottoman and perched gingerly on the edge. "I'm here to ask a favor."

Mason frowned.

"I know it's useless to ask you to move back to Lincoln. Where you belong. So I'll just ask you this. Come home for the month."

He retained his relaxed position even though every muscle bunched. "My work is here."

"According to your father there are at least three other people in the company who could do what you're doing here. Your cousin, Charles, for one. You remember him. The man sitting behind the desk formerly occupied by you. The man who took on your responsibilities when you selfishly indulged your rebellious streak. *Again*," she added with a fabricated sniffle of distress.

This is why he traded his position as second-in-command at RAVI headquarters for a sales and developmental position in the field. To escape the relentless guilt trips, the rigid expectations, and the life he'd never wanted. After five long years, he'd tired of filling his brother's shoes. It had never been a good fit. He'd forced it. For his parents. And, if he were brutally honest, for himself.

"Charlie was Jimmy's right hand man, Mom. He's qualified. He's motivated. He's family. The position should have gone to him in the first place. Not me. Just took me a while to do the right thing. Can we drop this now?" Mason shoved off the wall, fighting to compartmentalize a dozen emotions. "Are you hungry? Come on. I'll take you to lunch."

Rush, an Irish Wolfhound mix with a heart of gold, meandered into the living room, yawning and stretching, and giving Prissy the stink eye. In Mason's experience, dogs sensed when people weren't animal friendly. Or at least Rush always did. The big scruffy mutt gave her the cold shoulder and sat in front of Mason, thick tail thumping hard on the carpeted floor.

"I guess this means he needs to relieve himself," Prissy

said, taut face pinched with impatience.

"It means he wants to eat. I said the magic phrase. Or at least one of them."

"What phrase?"

"*Are you hungry?*"

This time Rush barked in answer.

Prissy raised a skeptical brow. "He was in the other room when you asked me that."

Probably sleeping on Mason's bed. Since they'd relocated, Rush had lapsed into a few bad habits. Sort of like his person. "A typical dog's sense of hearing trumps any humans," Mason said. "And Rush trumps a typical dog. He can perceive frequencies—"

"Don't go audio on me." Another one of her favorite sayings. She may have married a man who'd made a fortune developing and selling audio and video equipment, but she'd never understood or cared to learn the technical aspects or practical theories pertaining to the business. "Let's get back to the subject at hand."

Mason reached down and gave Rush's head an affectionate scratch. "Which is?"

She clasped her hands in her lap, sat rigid. She was beautiful in an icy sort of way. Easy to see why she'd caught Boyd Rivers' attention. When it came to women, the audio kingpin had a weakness for exceptionally attractive women. In that regard, and that regard only, Mason was a chip off of the old man's block.

"It's December," Prissy said. "You know how morose your dad gets around the holidays. How can you be so cruel?"

"Holidays are rough for a lot of people, Mom. Including me."

"So why spend them alone?"

"I'll join you for Christmas Eve and day."

"But—"

"My being there won't fill the gap left by Jimmy. Not for you. Not for Dad." Pride and temper reared its ugly head. "I'm done with pinch hitting for the favorite son."

Prissy paled.

Mason cringed. Not because he regretted the words, but because he'd spewed in anger. He was the one who'd allowed his parents to manipulate him. He was the one who'd suffered in relative silence for five freaking years. Distancing himself and starting anew wouldn't be easy but it didn't need to be messy.

Expression now eerily neutral, his mother stood and fussed with the buttons of her buttoned coat. "Lunch would be nice," she said in a detached tone. "That's if the offer still stands. I'll fill you in on family and local gossip. That is if you care."

"I'll grab my coat." Mason strode toward his bedroom, Rush walking alongside. For the Rivers, any sense of familiar warmth had died along with his brother. Things were always tense. But never more so than around the holidays.

God, what I wouldn't give for a little old fashioned Christmas cheer.

Mason nabbed his wool pea coat from the closet, snagged a gourmet biscuit from the treat jar on his dresser and tossed it to his loyal companion. "Do me a favor, Champ, and don't destroy anything while I'm gone." *Which of course you will. Even if it is just a piece of junk mail.*

That thought reminded Mason of the tickets he'd scored for this weekend's popular Mile High Christmas Extravaganza. He grabbed the envelope from his nightstand and tucked it in a drawer. Not exactly the kind of Christmas cheer his soul craved, but it sure as hell was a start.

* * *

Once upon the same night in Nowhere

Chrissy rolled into her driveway a half hour later than normal. Two back-to-back snowstorms had blanketed Dawes County in two feet of snow. The road crews had been diligent but the feisty and relentless winds wreaked havoc with plowed drifts, obscuring long stretches of country roads with the fluffy white stuff. That wouldn't be so bad, but the white stuff concealed the odd patch of black ice. Rather than risking an accident, Chrissy took her time on the drive home from work. She couldn't afford to trash her car. Or her body for that matter. She had Melody to think about. And damn if she didn't think about that kid all the time. Most recently, she'd been obsessing on their upcoming trip to Denver.

Melody was over the moon excited.

Chrissy was ramped to the max with dread. Her trepidation about running into Mason was equally matched only by Georgie's perseverance regarding procuring tickets for the Mile High Christmas Extravaganza. Yes, Melody would enjoy the visuals—the scenery, the costumes, the dancing—but she wouldn't hear one note of music. That grated on Chrissy's nerves along with the knowledge that she herself would be forced to suffer through every beautiful song played by the featured symphony.

Ever since she was a child, Chrissy had dreamed of making her living as a concert violinist. She had the gift. She had the training. But her passion for music died the moment the doctors pronounced her baby deaf. How could she enjoy what her daughter would never hear? She hadn't played her violin in almost five years and she'd shunned music in general, something her friends and family had respected for a while, but not so much this past year.

Nerves taut, Chrissy dumped her keys into her knitted slouch bag and squinted through the windshield at her tiny cabin home. Only six pm and already dark as the dead of night. Her kitchen window glowed with golden light and she could see her mom working at the sink. Probably washing dishes after making Melody supper. Or maybe they'd baked cookies together. Again. Even though Chrissy brought home a weekly sampling of the cookies she made at the bakery, Melody was all about the process of mixing up and decorating her own sugary delights. The thought of her daughter's sweet smile and endless effervescence prompted Chrissy to slap on a happy face as she looped her scarf around her neck and braved the frigid temps.

Her dad had shoveled and salted the path—just one of the perks of living in a guest cabin on her parents' ranch—but even so, walking without slipping was dicey. By the time she pushed through the side door and into the cozy kitchen, her smile was more like a crooked grimace.

"Rough drive?" her mom asked.

"A little tricky," Chrissy said as she stomped her boots free of snow. "Sorry I'm late."

"No problem. I made a meatloaf ahead of time. All your dad had to do was pop it in the oven. I should go though. He hates eating without me."

Chrissy didn't respond but her mind gushed with compliments and envy. Roger and Eva Mooney were two of the most loving and generous people she'd ever known and an adorable couple to boot. Crazy in love and forever devoted. Every so often they still acted like a pair of smitten teens. Chrissy had known that kind of giddy infatuation with Mason. Unfortunately, he'd tanked in the devotion department. Then again, Chrissy had fallen in love with a smooth-talking musician, a man only known to her at the time as *Romeo*. Bewitched by love at first sight, but committed to opposing dreams, they'd agreed to indulge in a fantasy, embarking on a week-long affair under assumed names.

What happens at the Oakley Festival stays at the Oakley Festival.

Only it hadn't.

"Melody's had her supper and bath," Eva said as she dried her hands on a dishrag. "She's in the living room, working on a holiday craft. She's really got the spirit this year, honey. We made snowball cookies earlier and she asked me to help her write a letter to Santa. Said my writing's prettier."

Wearing a festive bulky sweater that countered her now grim expression, Eva snagged an envelope from the counter and handed it to Chrissy. "She asked me to mail it for her, but I think you should read it first."

Scarf still looped about her neck, coat drooping off her shoulders, Chrissy opened the enveloped marked for a North Pole delivery. Her mom's expression suggested she was in for a shocker. Had her daughter asked for a big ticket item? Something beyond Chrissy's limited budget? Had she asked to hear, like other people? Or damn, oh, crud, had she asked for a daddy? As Mel had grown older, she'd become more confused about her single parent status. So far Chrissy had skated over the truth. Maybe those days were over.

Stomach churning, she unfolded the letter and read the content as dictated by Mel via sign language. She could easily imagine her daughter's tiny flying fingers.

"Dear Santa," Chrissy read aloud. "Grandma says I've been a good girl and good girls are on your nice list and that means I'll get presents. She told me to think hard and ask for what I want most. I thought really hard and I know what I want. It's not for me. It's for my mommy." Chrissy swallowed hard and blinked back tears. "She's always sad even when she's smiling. Instead of making her a toy, can your elves make her happy? Your friend, Melody."

"Tear jerker, right?" Eva asked as she pulled on her coat. "And I'm the one who heard it straight from Mel."

She paused, relieved Chrissy of the letter and envelope, then gave her arm a kind squeeze. "Leave it to my ever-starry-eyed granddaughter to ask for the impossible. Santa can't make you happy, honey. Nor is it something easily tackled by me or your dad or your brother, or even Melody. It's up to you to reconnect with pure joy. You remember that feeling, right? Pure joy? You used to sparkle with it. Like Melody."

She kissed Chrissy on the cheek then moved to the door. "Maybe Melody's note is a sign that it's time to stop depriving yourself of what you think you don't deserve. I won't tell you what to do," she said on her way out, "but dragging your fiddle out of the cedar trunk might be a good start. End of lecture."

The door closed and Chrissy stood shell-shocked as her mom headed toward the main house. She'd always gone out of her way to put on a cheery front for her daughter. Mostly it wasn't an act. No one made her smile like the light of her life. Either Melody was weirdly intuitive or Chrissy was more miserable than she'd realized. If she put bow to strings would she feel pure joy? Or only bitter regret for a forfeited dream? Was the lack of music in her life the root of her frustration? She didn't think so. Although she conceded it could be a contributing factor.

Chrissy eyed the platter of whimsical snowball cookies, feeling as bland as unflavored dough. "How does one find her happy?"

Leave it to my ever-starry-eyed granddaughter to ask for the impossible.

Chrissy flashed on another avid optimist in her life. A few months back, her cousin Bella had shot for the stars. Via an internet site, she'd literally applied for an impossible dream and, after bucking certain odds and utilizing a strong dose of derring-do, she'd made that dream come true.

Snagging her phone from her purse, Chrissy connected to the internet and pulled up the bookmarked site. Just as she had several times before, she read the whimsical come-on.

Impossible Dream.com
Making magic since 1956

Yearning for your dream job? Dream vacation? Dream home? Our data analysts and researchers pride themselves on working magic.

Chrissy wasn't the fanciful sort, but she'd been toying with applying to ID.com for weeks. She'd wrestled with the precise wording for the data form, something that would benefit Melody.

The wording was still up in the air, but the dream was suddenly and painfully clear. *Tonight,* she thought as she moved into the living room to bid her daughter hello. After she put Mel to bed, she'd fire up her laptop and fill out the application.

"Time to put stock in magic."

Three

Once upon a Winter Weekend

Wanting to believe in miracles and magic and having complete and unshakeable faith were two vastly different things. Bella had that kind of faith. Melody had that kind of faith. Chrissy had stared at the responding email and attached document from Impossible Dream thinking, *what the hell?*

Several nights ago, she'd spent two hours toiling over that extensive data form, sharing things about her life that she hadn't even shared with the Inseparables, with the exception of Sinjun. When it came to stating her actual dream, Chrissy kept it simple.

I want to find my happy. To feel pure joy. Not for a moment or a day, but forever.

On the one hand it seemed an unforgivably selfish wish. If asking for the impossible, why not ask that Melody be blessed with the gift of hearing? Honestly, that dream nipped at Chrissy's soul every day. But something about that wish hinted that Melody was somehow imperfect or unhappy—which she wasn't. She was simply audibly challenged.

More worrisome was the possibility that Chrissy's negative mindset and damaged spirit were weighing heavy on her daughter's heart. Knowing her cynicism might someday dull her daughter's sparkle was unacceptable. So in that regard her dream wasn't purely for herself but for Melody and everyone within Chrissy's beloved circle.

Attaining pure joy "forever and always" struck Chrissy as so farfetched that she'd expected ID.com to reject her application. She hadn't expected an affirmative response within a short span of three days. That's if you could call a confirmed reservation for concert tickets and a cryptic message as "affirmative".

Impossible Dream offers the most likely prospects based on data, research, and ID-tuition. It's up to the applicant to follow through. We provide the magic. You provide the derring-do. True passion and faith required. Patience recommended.

If she remembered right, it was pretty much the same message as received by Bella. And because of Bella, Chrissy knew that derring-do involved bold behavior. *Courage.* She'd never considered herself a wuss, so... Whatever it took. Bring it on.

True passion wasn't a problem because she was determined to succeed for Melody's sake.

Faith. That one was tricky.

Patience implied her path to "pure joy" wouldn't be an easy one. Which was pretty much a no brainer.

Still, she wished ID.com would have given her greater guidance. At least she'd made Georgie's day when she'd informed her of the supplied tickets.

"*I can't believe you got four tickets to the Extravaganza!*" she'd said. "*I've been checking back for weeks, hoping for cancellations.*"

"*Dumb luck,*" Chrissy had said.

Which was sort of true.

She couldn't imagine why Impossible Dream hooked her up with tickets to the Mile High Christmas Extravaganza, of all things. Was it because the musical portion of the program was being performed by the Mile High Symphony Orchestra? She'd boycotted live concerts, most especially those featuring orchestras, for the last several years. Would she find her happy by reconnecting with an experience that once stirred her soul? Maybe she'd have some sort of world-altering epiphany, accepting what others already believed. That Melody could enjoy musical performances, albeit in a different way. Or maybe the epiphany would result in realizing how fortunate she was to have a group of friends who'd gone out of their way to shine some extra love on her pre-birthday celebration.

Before she knew it their special weekend arrived. From the moment the Inseparables picked her and Melody up at the cabin, the day was upbeat and packed with surprises.

For her part, Chrissy shoved Mason from her mind thirty miles outside of Denver. She refused to obsess on a possible run-in. They were history. For crying out loud they'd barely even *been*. This weekend, she told herself as they rolled into the city, he didn't even exist.

As promised, Denver was decorated to the hilt—a bona fide Winter Wonderland. The *Blossoms of Light* display at the Botanic Gardens. The twinkling canopy of Larimer Square. The colorful and imaginative wonder of *Zoo Lights* at the Denver Zoo.

Spurred on by Melody's giddy joy, Chrissy relaxed into the getaway. The Inseparables plus One (but minus Sinjun) packed an impressive amount of delight into six dazzling hours. By the time they returned to the suite, Melody was down for the count, but the Inseparables partied on. Girl talk, boy talk, games, and candy cane shooters. Chrissy couldn't remember the last time she'd laughed so much and so hard. Sans the peppermint schnapps, it reminded her of their childhood slumber parties. Of younger days. Carefree days. It was as close as she'd come to pure joy in years.

Morning rolled around a little too fast but it didn't stop the girls from sightseeing and shopping their butts off. Between immersing herself in the festivities and abandoning her worries regarding Mason, Chrissy was beginning to feel a fraction of her old self. Spontaneous and fun. The best was when a performance artist—dressed as Jack Frost—broke out of a freeze pose and scared the stuffing out of Emma. Chrissy—who'd unfortunately just taken a sip of her warm beverage—laughed so hard, cider shot out of her nose. Unbelievably embarrassing, but totally worth Melody's unexpected and extremely loud belly laugh. As a child who rarely vocalized, Mel's laughter was music to Chrissy's ears. Knowing she instigated that laugh was a bona fide rush. In that moment, Chrissy sparkled.

Inspired, she floated on that glittery high all day, knowing it was directly linked to Mel's own sparkle. But now that they were standing in line at the performance center, hoping to buy two additional tickets via a last minute cancellation, damnable melancholy nipped at Chrissy's spirit. Once upon a time she'd dreamed of performing in a theater like this.

"I'm sorry Sinjun got bogged down with work and had to cancel on us," Georgie said as they shuffled closer to the lobby sales booth. "But at least it means we only need to snag two tickets instead of three."

"If we strike out," Emma said, "Angel and I vote to opt out. We'll shop and meet up with you girls after the concert."

"We're not going to strike out," Bella said. "Think positive."

"It's a miracle Chrissy scored four tickets to begin with," Georgie said. "We'll get two more. I feel it. This was meant to be."

There were only three people ahead of them now and, as they inched forward, Chrissy reached down to prompt Melody.

Only Melody wasn't there.

Chrissy whirled left, right, and all the way around. "Where's Mel?" Her daughter stuck to her like Velcro in crowded venues. She never wandered off. *Never.*

"What the..." Bella looked every which way. "She was just here."

"Holding on to the end of my scarf while I flipped through this damned concert program." Chrissy's insides twisted with guilt. *When did Mel let go? How could I not have sensed her absence?*

"Did she drift to the Nutcracker display?" Georgie asked.

"Bathroom?" Angel asked.

Chrissy's mind flashed with morbid scenarios. "Oh, God." Had someone snatched her daughter?

"Don't panic," Emma said as the women fanned out in search of a blond-haired, blue-eyed munchkin.

Chrissy frantically scanned the lobby as she pushed

through the crowd. Plenty of kids, but no Mel. Her pulse kicked into overdrive as she pushed outside. Icy wind blasted her face as she loped down the steps. Was Mel out here somewhere freezing and scared? *Stay calm, Christmas. Focus.* She wasn't sure if it was mother's intuition or the bright red coat, but Chrissy spied her daughter straight away. She was standing near the gargantuan decorated evergreen Chrissy had hustled her past because they were running late.

She would have been relieved except... A dark-coated man had Mel by the shoulders.

Every abduction headline she'd ever read propelled Chrissy across the snowy grounds at breakneck speed. "Get your hands off of my daughter!"

She was set to tackle the bastard to the ground, when he rose from his stooped position, hands raised in mock surrender. "Just trying to help."

He kept talking, his words garbling in Chrissy's frantic mind as she fell to her knees and pulled her daughter into a bone-crushing hug. Her mind gushed with relief and gratitude as she confirmed Melody's wellbeing. Mel was safe. And he—the man who'd been in her daughter's face—was still blathering. His words registered in fragments as the fog of panic faded around the edges.

"*Waiting for a friend... Noticed this little one... alone... lost... Didn't respond to my questions...*"

"It's because she can't hear," Emma, who must've been on Chrissy's heels, explained to the stranger.

Although, as Chrissy finally focused on his face, she realized the man wasn't a stranger at all.

Recognition was twofold. "I'll be damned," he said. "Juliet?"

Maybe the fact that they'd assumed the names of ill-fated lovers hadn't been the brightest idea. Although, it had seemed romantic at the time. Clutching Melody closer, Chrissy's heart squeezed. "I can't believe this."

"Me either." He dragged a hand through his shaggy brown hair, blue gaze locked on her face. He crooked a lopsided smile. "It's been, hell, almost five years."

She hated that her stomach fluttered. She hated that she was speechless. Mostly she hated falling in love at first sight for the second time.

"*This* is Benedict Romeo?" Angel asked.

"He-who-shall-not-be-named?" asked Bella.

"The dirtbag who—"

"Yes," Chrissy snapped, cutting off Emma. At some point all the Inseparables had circled. Rising now, she grappled for her senses.

She'd dreamed of this moment, a face-to-face chance to blast Mason for making a mockery of what she'd thought was an affair of the heart. For refusing to acknowledge his child. For threatening her family. She'd suppressed her hurt and fury for so long, but instead of blowing, instead of giving him hell, she reeled with a numbing realization. After all this time, after all he'd done, she still burned for this man.

What's wrong with me?

Acknowledging the group's hostility, Mason's pleasantly surprised expression morphed into one of confusion. "I seem to be missing something."

"What are the chances?" Georgie sighed. "Then again, just my bad luck. I knew I should've canceled this trip."

"I recognize you," Emma said. "Mason Rivers. Playboy millionaire."

He had the grace—or guile—to look sheepish. "Don't believe everything you read."

"I'm going by the pictures," Emma said with a crooked brow. "Your liaisons have been featured in the local tabloids more than a bed-hopping politician."

"An exaggeration. Trust me."

"How could you be such a jerk to my cousin?" Bella interrupted, red-faced. "Forsaking your daughter was bad enough, but threatening Chrissy and our family?"

"Whoa, whoa. What?" His gaze flew to Chrissy then down to Melody.

Chrissy swore she saw Mason estimating Mel's age, calculating the math. As if he didn't know.

He looked back to Chrissy. "What's going on?"

"Excuse us for bearing a grudge," Angel said, "but threatening our friend—"

"I didn't threaten anyone."

Just thinking about that certified letter, about that awful day, set Chrissy off like a firecracker. "Not directly, no. You relied on your father and lawyer for that."

Mason's nostrils flared, his stance went rigid. He glanced back to Melody.

Chrissy blinked. *He looks torn and, good grief, affected somehow by this.*

Rattled, she retreated a step, taking her daughter with her. Now that he'd seen Mel in person was he having second thoughts? Did he want to know her? To take her? *Stop thinking crazy, Christmas.* Only she couldn't.

Mason met her eyes, confusion and anger swirling in the charismatic gaze that continued to rock her world. "We need to talk."

In private was implied.

She couldn't make sense of his conflicted expression. Did he intend to reinforce his noncommittal stance? To make excuses for his asinine behavior? To offer support? To demand parental rights? A dozen scenarios welled—all of them troubling. Whatever his angle, she would not be finessed. Childish infatuation was no match for motherly love.

Chrissy maneuvered her daughter toward her cousin. "Please take Mel inside. I don't want her to miss the show."

Bella, champion of children everywhere, wrapped a protective arm about her niece while eyeing Mason and addressing Chrissy. "We're still short two tickets."

"I can help with that." Mason pulled an envelope from the inner pocket of his coat.

"What about the friend you're waiting for?" Bella asked.

"Canceled last minute." He fingered the envelope. "Two third row tickets. Center stage. You won't all be seated together, but you'll all get in. This show's been sold out for weeks."

"Tell me about it," Georgie said.

"How much do you want for them?" Angel asked, while opening her purse.

"They're a gift." Again, Mason focused on Melody. His expression softened. "The closer she sits to the stage, the more she'll feel the vibrations of the audio system."

Smirking, Emma snatched the booty from his hand. "The least you can do, right?"

"Maybe I should wait with you," Georgie said to Chrissy.

"No. I'm good. Thanks." She appreciated her friends'

support but this, whatever this was, was between her and Mason.

"Come on, sweetie," Bella said and signed to Melody.

Mel turned to Mason, smiled and signed.

"What did she say?" he asked.

"Merry Christmas," Angel translated.

Attention riveted on his daughter, Mason crooked a tender smile and returned the greeting, signing and saying, "Merry Christmas," then verbally added, "Cutie."

Four

He needed a drink. A stiff whiskey. A damned double.

He ordered coffee, black.

The last time Mason had felt this blindsided was the day he'd learned his brother had been killed in a car accident. But today, instead of losing someone, he'd found someone.

Two someones.

He didn't have it straight in his head, but he'd gleaned enough details to get the gist. It was possible, even probable, he had a child. The refreshingly frank and good-hearted violinist he'd fallen in love with wouldn't lie. On the other hand his father was capable of high level manipulation. If he had a hand in this, if he'd denied Mason a chance to know his own child, then a whole load of ugly was coming the old man's way.

One thing was certain. Juliet...Chrissy...was pissed.

Right now she was texting one of her friends regarding her whereabouts. He'd coaxed her into the coffee shop to escape the frigid cold. Even though the fury he'd felt rolling off of her had been hot enough to torch the holiday tree that had captivated her—*their*?—daughter's interest.

Melody.

He couldn't get her cute, impish face out of his head. A mini version of her mom. Milky complexion, pale blond hair, vivid blue eyes, and a smile that lit up the world.

"She can't hear."

That revelation haunted him as surely as her existence. He'd been living and breathing audio technology for most of his life. Maybe he could help.

Mind racing, Mason forced his thoughts back to the woman in front of him. She'd blown in and out of his life in the span of a week and earned a place in his heart forever. If it hadn't been for his brother...

Jimmy's death had changed everything.

Mason glanced at Chrissy's left hand. *No wedding band. Single then?*

"Sure I can't take your coat?" he asked as she pocketed her phone. He had a thousand questions. This could take a while.

"I'm sure."

She did, at least, loosen her scarf and remove her cap. Static electricity had her fine hair dancing like a halo.

Five years ago her hair had reached her waist. Now it was shoulder length and kind of choppy. Sexy. Like her full, pouty lips. Oh, yeah. He'd been a sucker for that mouth. Sometimes that week in Napa Valley seemed like a dream. Too good to be true. Too special to forget. Every look, every expression, every word exploded in his mind with vivid clarity.

"Chrissy, huh?" Starting with the basics, Mason loosened his tie and settled back in his chair. "That will take some getting used to. I wish I would have insisted on your real name before we parted."

"Would it have made a difference?"

Not immediately, no.

The day after they'd split up, he'd had second thoughts. Had racked his mind for a clue regarding the location of her school. But then he'd gotten the call. Jimmy wrecked his car, ending his life and, by extension, changing Mason's. Instant tunnel vision. His own needs and wants taking a backseat to his shattered parents. Later though, much later, yeah, knowing her name would have made a difference.

Her barbed mood chafed, prompting him to keep those thoughts to himself. Using aliases had been her idea. A college student at the time, she'd broken away from school to live it up for a week. To indulge in the various jam sessions and concerts at the Oakley Music and Wine Festival.

Mason had been in escape mode, too. Dodging his dad's attempts to lure him into the family business. Dodging a life he didn't want. Truthfully, it had been nice to be anonymous. For once he'd been able to trust that a woman was enamored with him and his talent, not his fortune.

Making a clean break at the end of that magical week had been her idea as well. In order to advance her lifelong dream, her parents—struggling ranchers—had invested heavily in her education. Veering from her chosen path wasn't an option. Plus, Mason had musical ambitions of his own, she'd said. The voice of logic. The voice of a woman with her own tunnel vision.

Still, he hadn't been willing to walk away without giving her the means to reconnect. He'd slipped her a card bearing his email address.

She'd never written.

Or had she?

"I know you're angry and maybe you have good cause, but bear with me...Chrissy. Whether you believe it or not, I'm in the dark."

"You're right. I don't believe it." She crossed her arms, narrowed her eyes. "When I found out I was pregnant," she said in an angry whisper, "I was shocked. We'd used protection."

"Except for that time in the shower and the—"

"I remember," she said, cheeks flushing.

"It only takes once," he said more for himself than her. And they'd slipped up twice.

"Sentimental sap that I was, I tucked away your contact info thinking, maybe someday. That day came sooner and for different reasons than I ever imagined. All I had was your email address," she said. "I thought you deserved to know. Thought you'd want to know."

"You're right."

"I didn't want anything from you. Didn't expect anything. But I sure as hell didn't anticipate learning you were the son of one of the wealthiest families in the heartland. I didn't expect a letter from your flipping family lawyer!"

So much for whispering.

Mason smiled at the waitress who stepped up, curbing his tongue until she'd served their coffee and stepped away. His heart pounded like a mother as he leaned in and focused on the only woman he'd ever loved. *God, she's beautiful.* Smelled good, too. Like holly or pine. Christmas scents. Scents that made him yearn and hope. "My father issues threats through our lawyer, not me."

"Even if that's true," she railed on. "Even if your father instigated that letter behind your back, the fact remains you chose not to respond to me personally. You made it clear that you wanted nothing to do with your baby. That hurt, but the threats and the insults were crushing. The Mooneys are not conniving money-grubbers. We don't give a damn about your millions."

Mason was getting more bent by the minute. "No wonder your friends think I'm a sack of—"

"They're protective."

"And I'm offended. You're accusing me of some royal douchebag behavior. I thought you knew me better than that."

"Are you serious? I don't know you at all! Our entire week together was a lie! I'm not talking about our names. I'm talking about our lives. I told you I was born and raised in a small town. That my parents run a modest ranch. That my older brother's obsessed with storm chasing. That I was preparing for a career as a concert violinist. Maybe I didn't give specifics like my name, where I was from or where I was going to school, but I was truthful about my background. You pretended to be a struggling musician, alone in the world and intent on landing a dream gig."

Mason worked his jaw. "I wasn't pretending. Listen. Let's put the anonymous aspect aside for the moment. Let's focus on Melody. If I'd known you were pregnant, I would have responded. I would have supported you, emotionally. Financially." He couldn't speculate beyond that.

She hugged herself tighter as if trying to hold it together. "The email—"

"I never saw it. Someone must have intercepted it, passing the contents on to my dad. I know it sounds lame, but that's my best guess. I'll get to the bottom of it, but for now, please, give me the benefit of the doubt."

Tears shimmered in her big blue eyes. "You're right. That sounds lame. But, okay. Fine. I'll cut you some slack. Maybe you didn't know. But now you do and I'm asking you to forget."

"What?"

"Don't press this issue with your father. He threatened to ruin my family if he ever heard from me again. If I ever contacted you... Promise me you won't mention today. This encounter. Our discussion. Promise you won't mention Mel."

Her panic sickened and infuriated Mason. "I can't do that." He wanted to pull her into his arms, to comfort and protect. Instead, he reached across the table and grasped her hand. "You wrote to me all those years ago because you thought I'd want to know I had a kid in the world. You were right. I may be five years late, Chrissy, but I'll be damned if I'll turn my back now on my daughter."

Her fingers and expression turned icy. "If you mean to sue for custody or even partial custody—"

"Don't insult me."

"We don't want your money."

"Understood."

"She doesn't know about you. I don't know how—"

"We'll figure it out."

She swallowed hard, shaking her head. "Why haven't you asked for proof? Don't you want a paternity test?"

Mason smoothed his thumb over the back of her hand, trying to ease a tension that rivaled his own. He looked into her eyes, remembering her passion and innocence and honest affection. "Is Melody my daughter?"

"Yes."

"Your word is proof enough." Along with my gut feeling. Together they set his life on a new course. Purpose infiltrated every fiber of Mason's lost soul. He couldn't remember the last time he'd felt this driven. This alive.

Chrissy licked her lips, tugged loose of his grasp. "You don't care that she's profoundly deaf?"

He'd wondered about the severity of her hearing loss. Now he knew. "Of course I care," he said, sensitive to Chrissy's defensive tone. *A lioness shielding her cub.* "And I have a lot of questions. But those can wait."

"If this is some misguided attempt... If you feel sorry for her, for me—"

"I feel sorry for myself. Melody seems like a great kid and I missed out on the first few years of that infectious smile."

Chrissy frowned. "I wish you'd stop saying nice things."

"Why? I'm a nice guy. If you'd think back, you'd remember that."

"I've been afraid that I romanticized that portion of my life."

"You don't trust me."

"I don't trust this. After all this time... You can't just waltz into Melody's life and play part-time daddy. You live here. We live in Nebraska. Even if we worked something out your father would never stand for it."

"Let me worry about my dad."

"While you're at it, worry about mine, too," she said as she stood. "He swore to kick your ass if he ever learned who you are. My brother swore the same. That's a double ass-kicking coming your way."

Mason stood as well, brow furrowed. "You never told your family my name?"

"I never told anyone. It wasn't worth risking your father's wrath." She pulled on her cap, hiked her hippy purse higher on her shoulder. "I need to get back to Melody."

"I'll walk you to the performance center."

"It's just across the street. I'll be fine."

He started to object, but she cut him off. "Please don't push this, Mason. I need time."

"I hear that. It's a lot to take in. For both of us. Is there someone in your life?"

She met his gaze and flushed.

"A boyfriend?" he prompted. "Fiancé?"

"Why?"

"Just wondering if I need to worry about a third ass-kicking."

She smiled a little and Mason's heart jerked just like the first time she'd smiled at him across the stage five years back.

"You're safe in that regard," she said.

No man in her life. That made things simpler. Something told him earning Chrissy's trust and his daughter's love wouldn't be so easy. Even though she was no longer staring daggers at him, she was still wary.

He tried to imagine her life for the last five years. A single mom of an audibly-challenged child and, by the modest look of her wardrobe, just getting by. Not to mention living all these years under the assumption that he'd rejected their daughter. Living in fear of his SOB father. Mason burned with anger and remorse, silently vowing to make amends. In the meantime his gut warned: *Tread lightly.*

Striving to end their emotional meeting on a lighter note, he snagged his phone from his pocket. "Considering we have a child together, this sounds ridiculous," he said with an awkward smile. "But could I get your number?"

She held his gaze for a tense moment then took his phone and punched in her information.

"I'll text you my number in return," he said, his brain revving on the future.

"I don't trust this, Mason."

"So you said."

"If you manipulate us, if your dad makes a stink, if you hurt Melody or my family in any way, I'll not only kick your ass, I'll make you sorry you were ever born."

Heart pounding with respect and, oh hell, lust, Mason took back his phone, his fingers lingering on her wrist.

Her pulse raced beneath his touch. Anger? Desire? He'd take them both. "I've been warned."

Five

Once upon a manic Monday
Nowhere, NE

"Here you go, Bryce. Two dozen chocolate chip, a dozen chocolate peanut butter, and a dozen holiday mixed cookies." Wired, Chrissy shifted from one booted foot to the other as she set the signature Buzz-Bee Bakery box on the counter and totaled the sale.

"Don't forget the cinnamon rolls."

"Oh, right. Half a dozen. Sorry."

"Make it a dozen." The rugged and quietly handsome owner of the Coyote Club, one of the two drinking holes in Nowhere, pulled two large bills from his wallet. "Breaking some bad news to the team tonight. Figure I'll soften the blow with sweets."

His team meaning his employees.

Chrissy's chest tightened as she imagined and yet another local establishment closing its doors. Rumors had been circulating for months. Bryce—The Bullet—Morgan, former pro football player, was on the verge of bankruptcy. If Coyote's went under, the people who lost their jobs would probably move away. As it was there were far more people than jobs in this dying town. "This news," she said as tumbleweed blew through her mind's eye. "Is it what I think it is?"

"Fraid so."

"Can't it wait until after the holidays?"

"Fraid not."

The servers, the bartenders, the musicians who played there every weekend—all unemployed, and right before Christmas.

Knowing her boss, Mrs. Wickham, was hovering in the background, and assuming the longtime resident of Nowhere would approve, Chrissy added three extra cinnamon buns— Buzz-Bee's specialty—to the mix. "Maybe something will happen before the midnight hour."

"What? Like a Christmas miracle?" His lip twitched as he scooped up the fragrant box. "Yeah. Well. 'Tis the season."

"Wait!" Chrissy called as he turned to leave. "I shortchanged you."

"Focus, Miss Mooney," Mrs. W admonished while emptying the dregs of the coffee urns.

Cheeks hot, Chrissy rectified her mistake. Her fourth mistake in the last hour. "Sorry, Bryce. I'm distracted."

"I know the feeling." Touching the brim of his hat in farewell, the gentle giant strode toward the door.

Like everyone else in town, Chrissy pretended not to notice his uneven gait. Plagued by a knee injury, that occasional limp was a reminder of his early and painful retirement from football. His reflexes, however, were still dead on. Proven when he dodged a direct hit as the door swung hard and Georgie blew in with an artic wind.

The woman tripped over her own two feet, face burning red as Bryce saved her—one handed—from a fall.

"Mind your step out there," she said without making eye contact. "It's really coming down."

Chrissy was pretty sure Georgie had tripped because she'd been flustered by Bryce—a long time not-so-secret crush—and not because she'd slipped on ice. Many moons ago Bryce had unintentionally stomped on Georgie's heart. She'd yet to recover from the rejection or the crush.

"Makes driving a bear," Bryce said of the storm as he stepped into the whirling flakes. "But it sure is pretty."

Chrissy marveled at the man's ability to retain his good

humor in the midst of disaster, wishing now that she would have paid for that box of sweets out of her own pocket. Even though the forty-ish athlete had flirted with fame and fortune, somehow he'd retained his downhome sensibilities. Ask anyone and they'd tell you The Bullet's monster financial problems were directly related to his overly generous heart.

Speaking of big hearts, Georgie, who was also swimming in debt, nearly blinded Chrissy with the blinking red-nosed reindeer pinned to the lapel of her coat.

"Please tell me you didn't buy that ridiculous thing," Chrissy said.

"Don't be a Scrooge," Georgie said then smiled. "Season's greeting, Mrs. W!"

"Same to you, Miss Poppins."

The gravelly-voiced, silver-haired proprietor of Buzz-Bee's squeezed in next to Chrissy. Though she was skinny as a rail and barely five-feet-tall, Mrs. W possessed an enduring don't-mess-with-me presence. Hence Chrissy hadn't commented on her garish gingerbread house earrings or the reindeer antler headband anchored over her black hairnet.

"I hope you don't want coffee," Mrs. W said. "I just swapped out the dregs for a fresh pot."

"Just stopped by to share some news with Chrissy."

"I hope it's good news. This girl's wound tighter than a ball of rubber bands." Mrs. W eyed Chrissy then spun around and resumed her coffee making.

"Love the antlers!" Georgie called.

"Of course you do," Chrissy muttered.

Grinning, Georgie tugged off the thick gloves Chrissy had knitted for her and lowered her voice to a conspiratorial whisper. "We're all set. Bella and Savage are expecting me and Melody for dinner. After that we're going to string popcorn garland and add more decorations to their tree."

"One more ornament and that spruce will tip," Chrissy said as she double checked the cash drawer. "Savage has got to be ODing on my cousin's festive cheer."

"I don't know. I think he's sort of into it. He even agreed to appear as Santa at the library."

For someone who'd suffered major issues regarding children due to his former job, Savage had come a long way since hooking up with Bella. Still. "Biker dude as jolly St.

Nick?" Chrissy snorted. "That I have to see."

"Take Melody to the Jingles Jamboree this week and you will." Georgie leaned over the counter and whispered, "Can you take a short break?"

"Go," Mrs. W said before she even asked.

Though somewhere in her eighties—no one knew for sure—the former school teacher turned confection maven had scary impressive hearing. "I'll just be a sec," Chrissy said.

Adjusting her knitted yellow skull cap which negated having to wear one of Mrs. W's cringe-worthy disposable hairnets, Chrissy followed Georgie to an empty table. Hugging herself as they passed the frosted panes of the store's front windows, she noted the heavy snowfall with a frown.

"Maybe I should reschedule this meeting with my parents," she said while they plopped in the yellow-cushioned seats. "This storm is hitting sooner than predicted. I'd hate for you and Melody to get snowed in at Savage's place."

"About that... Bella wanted you to know that if the talk goes badly with your parents and Zeke, if you need the rest of the night to decompress, Melody's welcome to spend the night with her. Same goes for if we get snowed in. We'll just make a party of it. Seriously, Chrissy. You've been living with this secret for five years. The sooner you tell your family about Mason, the sooner you can relax. You've been on edge ever since you ran into him. Not that I blame you. Your past history aside, the man is potent."

"Tell me about it."

"Gorgeous. Charismatic. Still into you."

"I don't know about that last part."

"You'd have to be dead not to notice. And if what he told you was true, if he really didn't know about Mel... If he wants to assume responsibility. If he wants to be a family—"

"Can we not go there?"

"Just saying I totally get why this guy haunted you for so long. He's—"

"Potent. I know. He's also stinking rich. An inheritance from his grandfather, trust fund from his dad, stock in the company. Not to mention his salary."

"That doesn't make him bad."

"But it does make him dangerous." Chrissy couldn't shake the possibility that Mason could rattle her stable world. If he fell in love with Mel... If he thought he could provide her with a better life... Knowing her parents, they'd have the same worry. And what about his father? What if Boyd Rivers made good on his threat?

Wired to the max, Chrissy drummed her fingers on the black-lacquered table. Her leg bounced with adrenaline-charged anticipation. The only reason she hadn't broken the news to her family the day she returned from Denver was because Zeke had been away for the weekend. She only wanted to tell this story once. Tonight was the night.

Meanwhile, two days after her run-in with Mason and Chrissy was still floating on a cloud of disbelief and a dollop of wonder. As jolting as that meeting and the subsequent conversation had been it had shifted her insides, altered her attitude. She had no evidence to back Mason's side of the story, but at least she had his side of the story. Until that moment she'd assumed the worst. That he was a serial womanizer who counted on his rich, influential daddy to clean up his messes. That he'd played her a fool that week in the valley. That he was a self-absorbed bastard who cared nothing about the well-being of his own child.

I care.

That one declaration had gone a long way, softening the fierce resentment she'd harbored for years.

I'm a nice guy.

One of the reasons she'd fallen so hard and fast for Mason in the first place. Her extreme bitterness had clouded that memory. But that same gentle kindness had been evident when she'd first seen him with Melody. And after, when he'd returned his daughter's greeting by mimicking her gestures— a palm sweeping twice toward the chest, followed by one "C" hand arcing, like tracing the top of a wreath.

Merry Christmas.

His effort had been clumsy, but sweet.

"Downplaying the lawyer's threatening letter is the key," Chrissy added as an afterthought. "The last thing I want or need is for dad and Zeke to confront the almighty Boyd Rivers. Rocking that yacht isn't smart. Allowing Mason to slip into our lives probably isn't the best idea either, but he made it clear he wants to know his daughter."

"You haven't said and we didn't want to pry," Georgie said, eyes sparkling with curiosity, "but I can't help myself. Has Mason contacted you?"

Chrissy's other leg joined in the anxious bouncing. "No. But it's only been two days and I did ask him to give me some time. Who knows? Maybe he won't call at all. Maybe he slept on it and decided he wasn't happy about being a daddy. Maybe—"

"Maybe he'll drop by on a whim," Georgie said.

"He lives in another state," Chrissy said. "Not around the corner."

But then she realized Georgie was focused on someone passing the window. Bells jingled signaling a new arrival. Chrissy knew even before she turned and made eye contact. The adrenaline that had been gushing through her body, spiked to her brain. She gave herself credit for not keeling over from a massive head rush as she stood and faced the subject of their conversation.

Mason stomped clumps of slush from his boots and shook snow from his hair, nodding to the proprietor in greeting before moving toward Chrissy. His stride was steady—unlike her pulse and legs. Her entire being zapped with sensual awareness. The other day he'd been dressed in a suit and tie—hot. Now he was dressed down in jeans and a thermal tee—also hot. He wore the same dark blue pea coat—nice—accentuated by a green cable-knit scarf with bright red tassels—hideous. Her fingers itched for her needles and a skein of sapphire blue yarn. Or maybe red—if he was shooting for festive.

"What are you doing here?"

"I was in the neighborhood."

She'd entered her name and number into his phone. She wasn't surprised he'd tracked her down, but she hadn't expected a surprise visit. Unsettled, she fell back on snark. "Went out for coffee and took a wrong turn?"

"I've been in town most of the afternoon. Before this I was in Lincoln."

Confronting his dad? Though Mason looked composed she did sense underlying tension. Had his father issued a nasty ultimatum? Had Mason relented? Rebelled? Or maybe

37

he was just anxious about forming a relationship with his daughter.

"Hey," Georgie said, moving in and breaking the awkward silence. "Georgina Poppins. Friend of Chrissy's."

"I remember," Mason said. "And before you jump down my throat, I'm not here to make trouble."

"Why are you here?" Georgie—God love her—persisted.

"To speak with Chrissy."

"Obviously," Georgie said with a smirk.

"Mrs. W?" Chrissy called.

"We're closing in an hour and you're as good as gone anyway, Miss Mooney, so go."

Grateful for the opportunity to speak with Mason before she spoke with her family, Chrissy smiled at her tough-as-nails boss then turned to her handsome-as-sin ex. "I can only spare an hour or so. I have a date. That is, an appointment. With my parents. And brother. I'm breaking the news. About you."

"Then my timing's perfect."

He smiled a little and Chrissy floated between besotted and annoyed. She'd never considered herself shallow, but she was enamored with Mason's good looks. His intelligent and kind blue eyes were her favorite feature, but every aspect—full mouth, chiseled jaw—was pretty much model perfect. Easy to see why she'd fallen into bed with him the first night they'd met.

Apparently few were immune to his charm. According to the media Mason had a stable of female admirers. She'd been one of many. Unfortunately that reality didn't temper her raging lust. That handsome face was only one part of the killer package. Add the charisma of a rock star and the talent of an accomplished musician, and, oh, yeah, she was a goner.

Georgie elbowed her, interrupting the drool-fest.

Cheeks burning, Chrissy cleared her throat. "I'll grab my coat. Maybe we can walk and talk."

"I should go," Georgie said to Chrissy. "You know where I'll be and who I'll be with, so call if you need us." Then she narrowed her eyes on Mason. "We protect our own."

"So do I," he said, with a tender glance at Chrissy.

"Huh." Georgie cleared her throat. "Right. Later then. Bye, Mrs. W!"

"Mind the icy roads, Miss Poppins."

Georgie hustled out and Chrissy hurried into the staff room before she did or said something stupid. Like moving into Mason's arms or offering to knit him a scarf. Too intimate on both counts. Mason's ability to warp her good senses was alarming. She'd damned the man to hell every day for the last five years and now she physically ached to lose herself in his arms.

What are you? A hormonal teenager?

Disgusted by her girlish infatuation, Chrissy talked herself down to earth. Buttoning her secondhand coat, she considered the rest of her appearance. Although her jeans and black tee hugged her petite figure, any sexiness was offset by her clunky sweater boots, the frilly yellow apron embroidered with a fat bumble bee brandishing a crooked, red spatula—Buzz-Bee's official logo—and her hand-knitted cap. Ten to one Mason was not fantasizing about getting up close and personal with her. Plus she smelled like cookie dough. Not exactly the perfume of a seductress.

"He's here for Melody, not you," Chrissy muttered to herself as she zipped out of the staff room, clipping poor Mrs. W and sending a cookie platter flying. "Crap! Sorry!" she exclaimed as the tray clanged to the floor and crumbs scattered. "Let me—"

"No. Go. Please," Mrs. W said with an exaggerated sigh. "You're a Nervous Nellie today, Miss Mooney. Whatever has gotten into you?" She shooed Chrissy away while glancing at Mason. "Don't answer that. I'll see you tomorrow. If roads permit."

Did Mrs. W just make an off-color crack? Chrissy couldn't go there. She muttered goodbye—she'd never muttered so much in her life—and hurried Mason out the door.

"Watch your step," two men said as they shoveled and salted the walk.

Chrissy recognized them as two employees of the nearby hardware store. "Thanks, guys."

"Anything for Mrs. W."

The frigid air both braced and chilled. Chrissy looped her thick, long scarf around her neck and tugged on matching mittens as Mason donned leather gloves—far more sophisticated than his ugly holiday scarf.

"Interesting character. Mrs. W," he clarified. "Is she always so formal? Miss Mooney? Miss Poppins?"

"Only with her former students. Velma Wickham taught elementary school for a hundred years. They had to boot her out of the place."

"And now she works at the bakery."

"My co-worker and boss. She owns Buzz-Bees," Chrissy said. "Inherited it from her son when he relocated to Florida."

"Given her age I'm surprised she didn't move with him."

"Mrs. W is a native and a lifer. Thank goodness. Her secret recipes have kept Buzz-Bees on the map. A lot of other businesses..." Chrissy fluttered a hand toward the random deserted stores. "As you can see, commerce is flagging. So," she hurried on, anxious to know his mind. "Walk and talk?"

Mason indicated the mounting flurries. "In this?"

More snow had already accumulated on the newly shoveled path. "I guess it could be dicey."

"And cold," he said, shoulders hunched against the wind. "Last time I looked the temp had dropped to the single digits."

Even though Chrissy's cheeks stung from the icy winds, she couldn't help but tease. "What are you, a wuss?"

"What are you, Nanook of the North?" Mason tugged her hat lower and knotted her scarf.

The easy banter and his thoughtful gestures catapulted Chrissy back to Napa Valley. She had to remind herself this wasn't the struggling musician she'd fallen in love with. This was Mason Rivers—millionaire playboy. She took a step back—physically and emotionally—and looked down the snowy sidewalk, scoping out a port in the storm.

"Are you hungry?" Mason asked. "I saw a café—"

"Café Caboose." She shook her head. "I'd rather not risk anyone overhearing us. In case you haven't noticed this is a small town. Everyone knows everyone's business, if given half a chance."

"If it's privacy you want, I can give you that. Ten, fifteen minute drive, depending on road conditions." He cupped her elbow and turned her toward a snow-covered SUV. "I'll drive."

She wasn't keen on giving over control. Plus, what if the storm worsened and she couldn't get back to her car? "Let's go separately. That way I don't have to backtrack." Before he could argue, she swung toward her own four-wheel drive. Tossing her purse in the car, she nabbed her long-handled scraper and attacked her snow-covered windows.

"Let me help," he said.

"I got it," she said. "You scrape your own so we can roll."

"You sure about this?" Mason asked as they made quick work of the powdery flakes. "I'd feel better if you rode with me."

"I've driven in worse storms than this. It's all fluff. Where are we headed anyway? The Sunset Diner on 20?" Although, the diner was north of town. He would have come in from the south.

"Your friend Angel's house," Mason said, ducking into his car before Chrissy could absorb and react.

How did he know where Angel lived? How did he know *Angel*? They'd only met briefly in Denver, right? And wait... Her new place or old? She'd recently moved. Although her new place was here in town. Fifteen minute drive, he'd said. Which meant her big house on Eagle Butte Road. The house she'd put up for sale. What... Unless... "Oh, hell no."

Putting her car in gear, she followed Mason down Frontier while digging in her purse for her phone. She'd vowed never to talk or text while driving, but curiosity overrode caution.

"Are you kidding me?" No juice. Zip. She was usually so good about keeping her battery charged and where the heck was the charger?

She dumped the contents of her purse on the passenger seat. Assorted personal belongings mixed with random toys of Mel's. Santa puppet, box of crayons, a pink pony with a braid-able mane. Everything but the kitchen sink and a phone charger.

"Crap!" What if her mom called? What if Mel needed her? Maybe she should veer off and head home. Then she remembered. Zeke had given her an extra charger last month. Glove compartment. "Yes!"

She plugged her phone into the adapter while keeping an eye on the road. Driving one-handed through a dancing curtain of snow was bad enough. A minute later she had enough juice to see she had three voice mails and a text from Angel.

Heart pounding, she braced and listened.

"Call me ASAP, Chrissy. You're not going to believe this. My realtor called and I... Well... Just call me."

Beep.

"I'm assuming you're slammed at work and I know how Mrs. W feels about personal calls on the business landline, so I thought I'd give your cell another try. Damn. Okay. And, cripes, he's here. Gotta go."

Beep.

"Just called Buzz-Bee's. Mrs. W said you left early. With a man. Assuming it was Mason. Call me when you can."

Anger welled, compromising Chrissy's senses and focus. Surely Mason didn't... Surely Angel wouldn't...

The one-sentence text left her hanging.

I hope I did the right thing.

As in selling her home to Mason? As in not selling her home to Mason? Chrissy itched to return Angel's call, to get the detailed scoop, but the snow was blinding. She needed to keep both hands on the wheel. She needed to focus. And besides she was only a few minutes from their destination.

"If it's privacy you want, I can give you that."

If Mason had the key to Angel's house then...

Chrissy lost it. She grabbed her phone and dialed the man in the car just ahead. "What have you done?"

"Get off the phone and focus on the road."

"Tell me you didn't buy Angel's house."

"I didn't buy Angel's house."

Chrissy's shoulders slumped with relief.

"I rented it."

Six

A game plan would've been nice. But it was too late for that. Mason had been flying by the seat of his pants for two days, driven by white-hot emotion and little else. His dad had stonewalled him on the phone. He'd stonewalled him in person. Flat-out denied any knowledge of a girl by the name of Juliet or Juliet Mooney or Chrissy Mooney or Christmas Joy Mooney. He claimed he didn't know about any email or pregnancy. *At least not that particular pregnancy.*

Over the years, a half-a-dozen girls had accused one of the Rivers brothers of putting a bun in their oven. All in an effort to milk the family fortune. Each and every one a false charge. At least Mason was in the clear. He couldn't swear the same for Jimmy. And, yes, all of those instances had been handled and swept under the rug by Boyd.

"*But not in this instance,*" the old man swore. He even got his lawyer on the speaker phone. Edward denied issuing a letter on Boyd's behalf to anyone in Nowhere, Nebraska. Then again, he'd swear the sky was green in order to protect his number-one client's privacy.

"*Did you see this so-called letter?*" Boyd asked Mason.

"No."

"*Then what the hell are you going on? Some chippy's word?*"

43

After that the conversation had deteriorated into full-blown ugly.

For once Mason had served the biggest blow.

This morning he'd driven away from Lincoln, discarding the family he'd been dealt and focusing on the family he wanted. West of North Platte he'd given into a whim, stepping up a plan he'd only partially researched. Instead of driving straight through to Denver, he took a major detour north, calling the posh doggie care where he'd kenneled Rush and booking an extra day.

Not wanting to give her a chance to shoot him down, he'd purposely steered clear of Chrissy while laying the groundwork.

I don't trust this.

Mason did.

Seeing her in Denver had triggered memories of the happiest week of his life. They were better than good together. They were magic.

Mason wanted magic. And he was pretty sure Chrissy needed magic. Gone was the vibrant free-spirit he'd made music and love with in the valley. Now she was subdued. Cynical and wary. He didn't want to believe he'd played a hand in shaping her new, troubled spirit. Either way, he was determined to reconnect with the maverick who'd roped his heart.

He'd rolled into Nowhere, a man intent on courting the mother of his child.

What have you done?

He was off to a rocky start.

He glanced in the rearview mirror for the hundredth time, breathing easier when he spied her headlights through the veil of thick flurries. She hadn't veered off. She hadn't spun out. He had to keep reminding himself that she was alert and used to driving in dicey weather. Just because his gut was tied in knots, that didn't mean disaster loomed.

The night Jimmy had spun out and wrapped his car around a pole, his judgment and reflexes had been impaired. Even if it hadn't been raining buckets, his chances of surviving that drunken joy ride unscathed had been remote.

"What a frickin' waste."

"*Mind your own ass, Slick,*" he could hear his brother

saying.

"Right. Thanks." Mason flexed his hands on the wheel and focused on his surroundings. He'd been pissed when Chrissy had called him while driving, but daydreaming was equally dangerous.

The narrow country road cut through miles of snowy plain, a vast stretch of frozen tundra peppered with the occasional ranch, random buttes, and clumps of snow-laden trees. A frosty wonderland that led to a warm, cozy house. A pricey three-bedroom home recently vacated by Chrissy's friend, Angel. Perfect for now and maybe even the future.

By the time he turned into the long driveway, he had to roll through five inches of newly fallen snow. Chrissy was right on his bumper.

He knew he was about to get an earful, but no amount of bracing prepared him for her fury.

She flew out of the car, mittened-fists pumping at her side as she stomped through mid-shin snow. "What do you mean you rented this place? Why? So you can blow in and out of Nowhere on a whim? Play daddy for the weekend? Once a month? Just because you have more money than God—"

"Not quite that much."

"—that doesn't entitle you to test us like a piece of intriguing audio equipment. If you like us, you invest more time and energy. If not, you kick us to the curb. I—"

He kissed her.

Fueled by white-hot emotion—*again*—Mason held Chrissy close and unleashed his passion. Frustration and longing mingled and burned. She tasted as sweet as she smelled. And—thank you, Jesus—after a moment's hesitation, she kissed him back with mutual enthusiasm. Passion ignited, she melted in his arms.

Heaven.

Or Napa.

At one time they'd been the same.

Reverting five years, Mason took familiar liberties, sliding his hands down her back and cupping her bottom. He finessed her against his car, pressing into her, losing himself in the wonder of brain-warping love. They burned—exactly as before. Before they'd parted. Before Jimmy's death. Before Mason had been sucked into the life he didn't want. Chrissy reminded him of who he'd been and who he could be.

She, this, *they*, meshed like the lyrics and music of a soul-stirring song. The perfect blend. A classic hit.

Magic.

But then she stiffened, breaking the spell with a soft push and startled expression. "Why did you do that? Why did you kiss me?"

Because I'm crazy about you. "Because I want you to remember who I am. Not the two-faced villain you've imagined me to be."

She averted her gaze and his pulse pounded with a dozen volatile thoughts. Nine freaking degrees and he was on fire. Physically. Emotionally.

"Yes, I come from money," he said, still gripping her shoulders. "Yes, I'm loaded and set for life. But that doesn't make me heartless or selfish. My dad is a controlling bastard. I'm not. My mom is pretentious. She's also a neat freak. I'm not. I still play guitar. I still like beer. I'm still looking to land that dream gig and—as you can tell—I'm still attracted to you."

She sleeved snow from her cheeks. Or were those tears? "We can't just pick up where we left off."

"That kiss said otherwise."

She looked at him then.

Tears.

Damn.

"Maybe you haven't changed," she said over the howling wind, "but I have. I have a child now."

"We have a child."

"What if you don't like her? What if she's too much of a challenge?"

"I won't dignify that with an answer." Mason thumbed away her tears, his heart cracking and swelling at the same time. God, how he ached to see his daughter. Her smile lingered on his soul like a cheery Christmas song. He knew he needed to take this slow. For Chrissy. For Melody. But that didn't make the waiting easier. "Come inside and let's talk."

Chrissy wiggled out of his arms. "No kissing."

The order lacked sting. Just like Rush. All bark, no bite. Mason's lip twitched. "Not unless you kiss me first."

"Dream on," she said while plowing through drifts to get to the porch.

"You can count on it." Smiling, he nabbed a shopping bag and his overnighter from the rear seat and then hurried ahead to unlock the door.

"I don't have much time," she said, moving inside the foyer ahead of him.

"I'll make this fast. Take off your coat. Make yourself at home. That's part of the reason I pushed so hard to get this place," he said while tweaking the thermostat. "It's familiar to both you and Melody."

She cast him an enigmatic glance while they hung up their coats and stomped snow from their boots. Was she intrigued? Touched? Creeped out and feeling stalked?

"How about some hot tea?" Heart pounding, Mason hurried into the kitchen, grabbing a kettle from the stove and filling it with water. Another perk. Angel had left the house partially furnished. According to her, the bulk of what remained had been purchased by her late husband. It wasn't really her style. It was also part of a life she wanted to leave behind. Mason had been in Angel's company for less than an hour, but long enough to learn a slice of her history. Long enough to reinforce what he'd suspected in Denver. Chrissy's close circle of friends was fiercely loyal. Which meant Chrissy was as special as he remembered.

"I thought Angel put this house up for sale," she said as she entered the kitchen.

She looked adorable. Those tight jeans and scrunched boots. The fitted tee and that fuzzy yellow cap. All she was missing was the apron. He had a sudden and erotic vision of Chrissy making cookies in this kitchen... wearing nothing but that frilly yellow apron. "Uh. She did. But she wouldn't sell it to me without speaking with you first. I pushed and she agreed to rent on a month-by-month basis."

"At least one of you acted rationally," she said while rubbing warmth into her arms. "Talk about an insane commute. Your job is in Denver."

"My heart is here."

"Stop saying things like that. It's so..."

"What?"

"Romeo." She frowned. "I can't believe we actually

referred to one another as Romeo and Juliet for an entire week. It was—"

"Romantic?"

"Ridiculous."

"It was your idea. Speaking of names," he said while searching the cabinets. "So your full name is Christmas? Christmas Joy Mooney?"

"My mom couldn't help herself."

He raised a quizzical brow while setting two mugs on the counter.

"I was born on December twenty-fifth."

"Ah." Mason smiled. "It's beautiful." *Like you.* "But you prefer Chrissy?"

"I'm not comfortable with Christmas."

"The name or the holiday?"

"Both." She moved to the stove, removing the whistling kettle from the burner as he rooted tea bags from the sack of groceries he'd purchased at the local store. "Let's get back to your job in Denver," she said while pouring water.

"I quit."

"What?"

"My dad insists on calling it a seasonal sabbatical. He thinks I'm having a life crisis. Says I'll realize where I belong once I calm down." He shot the woman at his side a meaningful look. "Could be the only time I've ever wholly agreed with the old man."

"Are you nuts?" She turned her back, clanged the kettle to the stove then spun back around. "I told you about the letter. About the threat. What if your dad blames me for you jumping ship? What if he lashes out at my family?"

"He won't."

"How do you know?"

"Because he'd only alienate me more. I made that clear. If nothing, he'll keep the peace for my mother's sake. The holidays... they're hard enough."

"I don't believe this." She hugged herself and shivered.

Because she was cold?

Or because he was too intense?

She had no idea how much he was holding back. The blowout with his dad had left him raw. That on top of adjusting to the news that he had a daughter, plus realizing he was still crazy about Chrissy. Yeah. He was wired and edgy. Impatient and maybe a little irrational. "It's drafty in here. Let's have our tea in the living room."

She glanced at her watch.

"I know. You have a date with your family. That's why I'm going to step things up."

Since Angel had given him the nickel tour, Mason navigated the house with relative ease. The living room was one of his favorite rooms. Spacious, yet cozy. Dark wood and a cobblestone hearth. A huge bay window with a view of the surrounding fields and a distant butte. A red leather sofa and matching club chair. He'd already scoped out a wall for a mounted plasma HDTV and a corner for the biggest Christmas tree he could buy.

Remembering the way Melody had been entranced by the decorated showpiece at the performance center, he made a mental note to purchase an abundance of twinkling lights and sparkly ornaments—as well as a collection of closed-captioned movies. Even if she couldn't read the words just now, she'd be able to read them later. It was all about planting seeds with kids, right? For now it was festive background for decking the halls. Just thinking about helping his daughter decorate the tree while watching holiday favorites turned Mason's insides to mush.

"I'm not one for sharing my darker thoughts," he said while settling next to Chrissy on the buttery leather sofa. "But I want you to understand my motivation."

"I'm listening," she said, even though she looked like she wanted to bolt.

Mason soothed his tight throat with a sip of tea then set aside the mug. "Back in Denver you accused me of being cagey about my background during our time together. You assumed it was because I was playing you. Thing is, I'm the one who's used to being played. Women who know who I am are usually more interested in the family fortune than in me."

"If I'd known who you were, about your fortune, I would have run the other way."

"Then I'm especially glad you were in the dark. That week with you was the highlight of my life."

"I find that hard to believe."

"I know you do. That's why I'm cutting open an emotional vein."

"I—"

"Let me get this out." Mason braced his forearms on his knees, clasped his hands together and bled. "Where my family's concerned, I've always felt like an alien. I don't take after my mother or father and I'm..." He faltered, unhinged as always when he thought of Jimmy. "I was the opposite of my brother. More than once I wondered if I was adopted. I even asked."

Chrissy's brows rose.

"I wasn't. Luckily, my parents didn't give me too much guff for doing my own thing. They tolerated my rebellious years, as my mother calls them. I didn't want to sell audio equipment to rock venues. I wanted to play those venues. Little compares to the adrenaline rush of performing live on a stage. Connecting with the music, the audience."

Chrissy glanced away and Mason flashed back on those jam sessions at the Oakley Festival. Remembering how she'd dazzled listeners with her inspired solos. "Not that I'm telling you anything you don't know," he continued, wondering at her pained expression. "Anyway, I managed to live that dream for a couple of years with little interference from my parents. Until they lost Jimmy. My older, and only, sibling. Then they turned all their attention to the second son."

"I remember reading about the accident," Chrissy said, her expression softening. "It happened—"

"The day after you and I split off."

"At the time I didn't know you were related. That you were a Rivers. Were you and your brother close?"

"Yeah." Mason ignored the ache in his chest. "Losing him sucked. And the way he died..." Mason shook off the memory of his brother's mangled body. "It was devastating. I wasn't thinking clearly when I returned to the Rivers fold. Chasing after you got stuffed to the recesses of my mind along with any thoughts of my own happiness. I wanted to ease my parents' suffering. I wanted to honor my brother by keeping his dream alive."

"Which involved working for your dad."

"Maintaining and building the success of RAVI." Mason dropped his head, cursing the day he'd sold out. "I tricked myself into believing this was my chance to finally bond with my parents and I spent five years perpetuating that notion. Last spring, I hit the wall. How could I bond with two people I didn't even like? If I were to salvage any sense of family, I knew I had to distance myself. I stepped down from my corporate position and moved to Denver to work as an audio analyst and engineer. Scoping out clubs, testing gear, initiating deals." He met her gaze. "What did you think of the sound system at the performance center?"

Chrissy blinked.

"Designed and installed by RAVI. Everyone who mattered seemed pleased. Hence those two third-row tickets. Just one of the perks of the job."

"Oh. I thought maybe... Never mind."

Mason frowned. "What?"

"No. It's silly. Go on." Holding the mug between both hands, she drank tea and relaxed into the puffy accent pillows.

Progress? Mason took heart and pushed on. "I was restless in Denver. I've been restless for years. You crossed my mind more than once, trust me. You were so set in your goal and so crazy talented, I assumed you were touring with a company or committed to a metropolitan orchestra. Probably swept off your feet by some other lucky SOB. Since I never heard from you, I chalked up our time together as a wonderful, but ill-timed affair."

He took a breath, fought to slow his thoughts. "I seriously thought we were history, hon. That I'd blown my chance. After running into you in Denver... After the latest confrontation with my dad... I decided to quit working for RAVI. I still have stock in the company. I'm still the heir, unless Dad changes his will. But I'm no longer an employee. I'm a free agent. Moving to Nowhere was a no brainer."

"But there's nothing here."

"You're here. Melody's here."

"So you chuck your career—"

"A career I didn't want."

"Ditch your home in Denver—"

"A rented condo. There's nothing for me in Denver. Except my dog, Rush. You're not allergic to dogs, are you?"

"No, but—"

"Melody?"

"No. I—"

"Good. Rush is going to love this place. Room to run. And he loves kids. He'll be good with Melody. Might even be good for her. Have you ever heard of Hearing Dogs?" Mason sat straighter, his thoughts tumbling over one another as he scrambled to prove his sincerity. "Comparable to a Seeing Eye Dog, except they're trained to alert their person of household sounds, things that help to ensure everyday safety and independence."

"I've read about them, yes."

"Rush isn't trained, but if Melody feels comfortable with him, maybe that's an avenue we could explore. I did a little research. Hearing Dogs are trained to respond to certain sounds. Honking horns, fire and smoke alarms, the telephone, oven timer, alarm clock, door knocks—"

"I know. I've researched, too. I research all the time, Mason. Resources and products for the hearing impaired. Education and advancement in technology. Just because I'm a single parent, just because I'm limited financially, that doesn't mean—"

"I know you're doing everything in your power to provide Melody with the best of care. I know that," Mason said, "because the girl I fell in love with had a kind heart and fiery determination. I'm just sorry I wasn't in the picture affording back up. I didn't mean to offend. I'm trying to help and I'm five years behind the game so my freaking brain is racing to close the gap."

Frustrated and emotionally drained, Mason dragged his hands down his face. "Guilt's a bitch. But it pales in comparison to gut-wrenching regret. I should have followed you back to school that day. I should have asked you to marry me. God knows, I've never loved anyone the way I loved you."

Visibly shaken, Chrissy blew out a breath. "What am I supposed to say to that?"

He held her gaze, reached over and grasped her hand. "Say you'll give me a chance. Give us a chance. As in you, me, and Melody."

"And Rush?"

He smiled a little. "Yeah. And Rush."

She looked down at their entwined fingers. "Melody's going to love you."

"I hope so."

"That worries me. If this doesn't work, if you decide to bolt, if your dad makes trouble... A hundred and one things could go wrong."

"All we need is for one thing to go right. Us."

She raised one brow. "'Tis the season for miracles?"

"Taking a leap of faith never seemed more right."

"We provide the magic." *You provide the derring-do.*

He scrunched his brow.

"Never mind." She smoothed her thumb over the back of his hand. "How would you feel about meeting my parents?"

Mason smiled.

Seven

Chrissy pressed closer to the frosted living room pane, hugging herself against a chill as she watched Mason shoveling drifts of snow. He'd insisted she stay inside while he attacked the worst of the mounting barricade. Between the blowing flurries and the darkening skies, she could barely make him out.

He'd been at it for a good fifteen minutes. She had to confess she was impressed by his strength and stamina and dogged determination. She'd always considered him more of an artist than an outdoorsman. Apparently, he was both.

The chivalry thing was hot, too.

Everything about Mason Rivers—except for that hideous holiday scarf—was hot. She had to wonder about the women who cared more about the wallet than the man. Clearly they were shallow with a capital S.

Chrissy was only a little shallow. She didn't care about Mason's wealth, but she was fascinated by his handsome face and smoking body.

She was also over-the-moon charmed with the man. Knowing he'd considered chasing after her, even after she'd been adamant about breaking up, was a seductive thrill. The giddy out-of-body sensation was a clear indication of her besotted state. It wasn't the same as "pure joy", but it was damn close. So close that her mind flew to Impossible Dream.com.

Her request: *I want to find my happy. To feel pure joy. Not for a moment or a day, but forever.*

Their reply: *We provide the magic. You provide the derring-do.*

Was Mason the magic?

ID.com had supplied her with tickets to a sold-out concert. Tickets that had ultimately led her to Mason.

What were the chances?

By fate or design they'd been reunited, and now Mason was desperate to turn back time and fast forward all in one miracle-making swoop. Chrissy felt like the unwitting star of a Hallmark movie. Unfortunately, given her jaded temperament, 'too good to be true' kept drowning out thoughts of 'lucky me'.

"Take a freaking leap of faith already," she mumbled to herself. "'Tis the season for miracles. Georgie said so. Bryce said so. And so says the majority of the population."

Even though Chrissy tended to keep her innermost conflicts to herself, she had a sudden and fierce urge to sort through her jumbled thoughts with a friend. Although she felt equally close to all of the Inseparables, in this instance she reached out to Sinjun. Given the fact that Chrissy was so private, confiding in their long-distance friend, someone she didn't interact with on a daily basis, came easier. Plus Sinjun was weirdly intuitive and Chrissy was desperate for dead-on advice.

As the phone rang, she paced the length of the picture window, drumming up body heat and working off adrenaline. When Sinjun answered, Chrissy almost whooped in relief. "Am I calling at a bad time?"

"Just going through some files," Sinjun said. "I could use the break. I'm glad you called. I know I texted before and I know we had that group video chat after you ran into Benedict Romeo, but I really am sorry about bailing on the Christmas birthday bash."

"We missed you," Chrissy said honestly. "It's been far too long since we've seen you in person, but of course we understood. Although I have to say your boss, whoever he is, is a real taskmaster. Do you ever get a break?"

"What can I say? I'm good at what I do. So what's up with you? I'm guessing this has to do with Mason?"

Chrissy marveled at Sinjun's ability to, once again, gloss over her exact "job". Bella often mused that Sinjun worked for the government, some sort of covert position that necessitated complete secrecy. That seemed farfetched to Chrissy although there was definitely something wonky about the way Sinjun consistently diverted attention away from her own life.

"Mason's moving to Nowhere," Chrissy said, cutting to the chase. "In fact, I'm with him now. Actually, he's outside shoveling snow. And I'm in here going slightly bonkers."

"Where's here?"

"Angel's house. Her old house. The one she shared with Baxter. Mason wants to buy it, only Angel balked, so he settled for renting. He has to go back to Denver at some point to pack up his belongings and his dog, but it's a done deal, Sinjun. He quit his job. Took a stand with his dad. He wants to pick up where we left off. He wants me. He wants Melody. He wants... a family."

"What do you want?"

"I want...magic. I want to reconnect with the old me. The me that sparkled. I didn't tell you this before," Chrissy said while wearing a path in the carpet, "but Mel wrote a note to Santa. Instead of asking for a toy, she asked if his elves could make me happy."

"That's intense."

"Tell me about it. I reacted a little out of the norm by writing a letter of my own. Sort of. Remember that internet site that Bella applied to a few months back? The site that matched her up with Savage? In a moment of madness, I applied for my own impossible dream. I applied for "happy". Can you believe it?"

"Well, I—"

"A few days later I got an email from datawiz at impossible-dream-dot-com, relaying that same cryptic message they sent to Bella."

"Magic, derring-do, passion and patience?"

"Exactly. Plus tickets to the Mile High Extravaganza."

"Which took place in Denver where you ran into Mason who you hadn't seen or spoken to in five years. So, what? You think Impossible Dream set up your reunion?"

"What if Mason is the key to my happiness?"

"True happiness, pure joy," Sinjun said in a soft voice, "comes from within."

"I know that."

"Do you?"

Chrissy nibbled her thumb nail as she faltered in her steps. She stared out the window, locking onto Mason's shadowed form. Her heart pounded as she vocalized her thoughts. "Something happened to me in Denver, Sinjun, and it started with Mason. Yes, our reunion got off to a rough start, but clearing the air lightened my spirit. I experienced a twinge of full-blown happy after leaving him at the coffee shop. He not only shared his side of the story, I vented my pent-up outrage then took a stand. The relief was immense.

"The second twinge of happy occurred when I returned to the performance center, when I traded places with Bella and settled in the seat next to Melody—third row, center stage. The concert was in full swing and Mel was fully engaged. Blue eyes wide with wonder and smiling ear-to-ear, she remained riveted for the next hour.

"Sitting close to the stage intensified the splendor," Chrissy went on as she relived the moment. "Mason had been right about the vibrations. They were pretty intense. And because Mel's other senses compensate for the lack of hearing, she was probably even more sensitive to those vibrations than me. Something inspired Mel to dance in her seat and it wasn't the melodic or lyrical aspects of the orchestra's holiday repertoire."

"That must have been thrilling to see," Sinjun interjected.

"It was," Chrissy said. "I didn't fully get it, so I mentally muted the sounds—the voices, the instruments—and tried to experience the event through my daughter's silent world. Even dismissing the lively and exquisite music, the festive visuals—scenery, costuming, choreography—were delightful and sparked my own sense of childlike wonder. Maybe Mel's shimmying was inspired by the movement of the professional dancers as opposed to feeding off of the vibrations from the audio system." *An audio system installed by Mason and RAVI.* "Still..."

Mel's uncoordinated chair dancing had been a game

changer for Chrissy. She'd known at that moment that she had to conquer her aversion to music, or at least curb it. Depriving her daughter of concerts and festive dances was no longer an option. Yes, Chrissy had experienced deep melancholy when she'd homed in on the orchestra's string section, but that was her problem, not Mel's.

In another life, in her childhood dreams, that could have been Chrissy on that stage, seducing the strings with her fingers and bow. Wooing the world with heart-stirring song. Instead she'd chosen motherhood over a demanding career. And then later, she'd turned her back on music altogether. Again, *her* choice.

'*The grudge*', as her friends called it, was born of resentment and bone-deep sadness and had little to do with Mason Rivers. She knew that now. Maybe she'd known it all along. Blaming Mason for the bulk of her misery had been easier than facing her inner demons.

"Mason still plays guitar," Chrissy said. "He still lives and breathes music whether he's designing audio systems or sitting in with a band. On top of that he's a tech head and he's loaded—not that I care, but it's a bonus. If anyone can enrich Mel's life, it's Mason. Plus he has a dog. A dog and a daddy for Christmas. Mel will be in heaven."

"And that will make you happy," Sinjun said.

"Yeah," Chrissy said with a convinced nod. "It will." Impossible dream granted. She started to say something more but paused when she heard another female voice snapping at Sinjun in the background.

Sinjun excused herself a minute then came back with, "Can I call you back later, Chrissy? I'm sorry but...duty calls."

"I don't think I like your boss."

"That makes two of us."

Chrissy frowned. "No need to call me back tonight. Unless you need or want to talk. You know. About you and your life?"

"Just remember what I said about happiness," Sinjun said before signing off.

"It comes from within," Chrissy said, wondering now about her friend's quality of life. Pensive, she slid her phone in her back pocket and returned to the window. A motion detector light had flickered on and now the futility of

Mason's efforts was clear to see.

Even so, he continued to shovel.

All because she'd invited him to meet her parents.

He had to know the introductions would be tense. She'd even warned him about the ass-kickings potentially coming his way. He'd simply promised to do his best to smooth things over.

"I'll be damned if I'll fumble this second chance," he'd told Chrissy before venturing into the storm.

"Are you my path to pure joy, Mason?" *Or merely a pleasant distraction?*

They came from different sides of the tracks—rich boy, poor girl—and when did that ever work out on a forever-and-always scale? Unlike Bella, Chrissy had little faith in real-life fairy tales. Regardless, Chrissy had been floating on a cloud of highly intoxicating infatuation ever since she'd reconnected with Mason in Denver.

When he'd walked into the bakery she'd felt a full-body zap.

When he'd pulled her into his arms... That kiss, that amazing four-alarm kiss, had catapulted her back to Napa, back to their fantasy week, back to the girl she'd been before harsh realities bitch-slapped her zest.

That kiss rekindled her lust for life and his subsequent baring-of-the-soul reinforced her love for the man.

Given Mason's happy-go-lucky nature, she'd been shocked to learn of his emotional hardships. Apparently even rich boys had baggage. Chrissy couldn't imagine feeling like an outcast in her own family. Or being looked over in favor of her older brother, Zeke. She didn't have a lot of money, but her life was rich with family and friends who loved her for who she was, even on her grumpiest or most rebellious days.

She couldn't blame Mason for wanting what she had—a warm and loving family. On the other hand, the pressure to fill a void in him was daunting. Especially given her own discontent.

Two seconds from calling Mason in from the storm, her butt rang, prompting her to snatch her phone from her rear pocket. She'd already gotten a text from Georgie letting her know she and Melody were safe with Bella and Savage, so it had to be Angel. Only it wasn't.

"Hi, Mom. Is everything okay?"

"Yes and no. Everything's fine here, but there's a problem with the windbreaks at the Morgan Ranch. As you know, Arlo is shorthanded and Bryce is stuck in town. Your dad and Zeke rode over to help. Only a small portion of the herd is at risk, still... If this storm turns worse..."

"Don't borrow trouble, Mom. Dad's a top-notch cattleman and you know Zeke in storms. Fearless, competent, lucky." Even so Chrissy's pulse kicked.

"You're right, of course, dear. The men will be fine. The livestock will be fine. This storm doesn't compare to that catastrophic blizzard two years back. Nevertheless, it's disrupting. I'm sorry, dear, but we need to reschedule the family meeting."

"Another day won't make a difference," Chrissy said, hoping she didn't sound as disappointed as she felt. "I'm running into some weather-related issues myself."

"Are you still in town? On the road?"

"I'm at Angel's."

"Good. Stay there. Spend the night and enjoy your friend's company. Melody's safe with Bella and Georgie. You stay safe with Angel. Do not drive in this storm. I'm worried enough about your dad and Zeke. Promise me you'll stay put."

She glanced out the window and saw Mason throwing in the towel. "I promise. But Mom—"

"Don't worry. I'll let you know as soon as your dad and brother are home safe. Meanwhile I'm on pins and needles wondering what you need to talk to us about. I know you were thrown by Mel's letter to Santa and I know I added an element of pressure by bringing up pure joy. I have to ask, sweetheart, is this about your music?"

Heart pounding, Chrissy moved toward the door as Mason moved toward the house. "No, Mom. But it is about passion."

"Oh. I... Is this about a man? Are you seeing someone? Oh, Christmas, honey—"

"I really don't want to talk about this on the phone."

"How serious is it? Is it someone we know? Someone you just met?"

"Mom—"

"I know. Not on the phone. I'm just so glad it's something good. I won't say a word to your dad. I'd rather he hear it from you. Enjoy your evening with Angel, honey."

The call ended before Chrissy could correct her mom on several counts. She chalked it up to a blessing in disguise. Her mom had enough worries with her husband and son braving the elements to save another man's cattle. She didn't need to know Chrissy would be spending the night with her former lover instead of her longtime girlfriend. She didn't need to fret about the unexpected intrusion of her granddaughter's father. Not now at any rate.

Chrissy pocketed her phone as the door swung open and Mason stomped in, red-faced and winded.

"What the hell?" he snapped. "I checked the weather this morning. This storm was a full day out."

"We're talking about Mother Nature, Mason. Not always predictable. Ask my brother some time. On second thought, don't. He's got more stories than a library."

"You're not going to like this," he said while shrugging off his snow-crusted coat.

"We're snowed in."

"I managed a path, but it's still coming down and the road's a mess. I'll get you home—safely—but not on time."

Thoughtful. Bold. Caring. She wanted to hug him, dammit. Instead she folded her arms and backed away so he could move out of the chilly foyer.

"A noble offer," she said as she backed into the living room, "but unnecessary. My mom called and canceled our meeting. My dad and brother are tied up at a neighbor's plus she doesn't want me on the roads. She told me to stay put."

Mason raised a brow while rubbing warmth into his hands. "Where does she think you are?"

Chrissy flushed. "I told her I was at Angel's house and she just assumed I meant her new place in town."

"She thinks you're with Angel."

"I didn't correct her because I didn't want to explain about you over the phone."

Hands on hips, he angled his head and frowned. "So we spend tonight in secrecy? Just like that week in the valley?"

The back of her knees connected with the couch, making her feel trapped. She hugged herself tighter and raised a defiant chin. "It's not the same."

"It feels the same. Like we're sneaking behind their backs. I don't like it."

Something about his exasperation tempered her own. She blew out a breath and closed the space between them. "We're not sneaking behind their backs. We're saving them from a restless night's sleep. As soon as my mom learns who you are, she's going to consider your family's wealth and all sorts of potential ramifications. She's already worried about my dad and brother and Mr. Morgan's livestock. I didn't want to give her anything more to obsess on. Not tonight."

She gazed up into his eyes, her heart and mind skipping back to the most breathtaking week of her life. A spontaneous break from her then intensely structured studies. Mason had seduced her with easy charm and wickedly impressive musicianship. She'd fallen hard and fast and apparently forever because her most fervent urge right now was to kiss him into tomorrow.

"Let's look at this storm as a Godsend," she plowed on. "A night to ourselves to sort things out. To talk and… I don't know. Get to know one another again. Only full disclosure this time. I know you're trying to make up for lost time, but it's too much, too fast. You, us, now—it feels like a fairy tale, like that week in Napa. In the long term, I need real. Melody needs real."

Mason smoothed his hands over her shoulders then gently pulled her into his arms. "How's this feel?"

"Cold," she answered honestly even as she melted against him. "You're a block of ice, Mason."

"I can think of a thing or two to warm me up."

"I bet you can."

"One would involve kissing and you said—"

"I take it back." She cradled the sides of his gorgeous face and pulled him down for a tender kiss. As soon as their mouths fused, she burned. Tender had been a nice thought, but deep and hot came naturally.

Chrissy gave over to the passion, the need and longing, and the sheer wonder of kissing the man who owned her soul. The father of her child.

This kiss shattered the last of her resistance and summoned whimsical images of elves gluing together broken dreams and sewing the tattered fabric of happy.

When they broke for air, Mason dropped his forehead to hers and she placed a hand to his chest. His heart pounded like a tympani drum against her palm. "How did that feel?" he asked in a tone that seduced her senseless.

Chrissy's heart sang. "Real."

Eight

He was heading up the stairs as she was coming down.

"Did you video chat with your cousin and Melody?" he asked. "Everything okay over there? Electricity? Heat?"

"Yes, yes, yes, and yes." They met midway in the stairwell, electronic tablets in hand, Chrissy one step above Mason. "What about you? Were you able to check in on Rush? Is he okay?"

"Yes and yes."

She glanced over her shoulder. "It's cold up there."

He jerked a thumb. "It's cold down there. Something's up with the heater. Obviously. I checked it out but I'll be damned if I can pinpoint the problem."

"No wood for the fireplace downstairs," she said. "But upstairs..."

"What?"

"You didn't notice? Master bedroom. An electric fireplace with a heater. Angel's always cold. Thin blooded, I guess. Baxter, her second husband, installed that luxury for her comfort."

"Sounds like a nice guy. I'm thinking we should take advantage of his generosity."

"I'm thinking the same."

"I bought food and wine," he said. "I'll run down and

bring up dinner."

"I'll fire up the heater."

They split off without another word, but Mason's mind raced ahead.

Bed, wine, a romantic fire. Who cares if the flames are artificial? She just invited me to crash in a bedroom. The only room with heat. Which means she essentially invited me to sleep with her.

At least that's where Mason's head went.

"You're thinking with your dick, bro."

Mason wasn't sure whether that was his conscience or Jimmy talking. Either way, he couldn't argue. "Turn it down a notch, Rivers."

He deliberately slowed his pace. Tripping over his own two feet in haste and breaking his fool neck was not the preferred next scene in this unfolding saga. Enchanting Christmas Joy Mooney, his one true love and the mother of his child, was the preferred next step.

She wanted real. He wanted magic.

"Real magic," he said to himself while gathering food and drink. "Maybe I should write a letter to Santa. All I want for Christmas is a wedding in Nowhere."

Whoa.

He paused, stunned by the clarity of that spontaneous realization. He wanted to marry Christmas Mooney. No deep thought. No hesitation. A natural progression in their whirlwind, albeit inconsistent, affair. He'd been an idiot, allowing five years to slide by, assuming she'd gone on her merry way, landing a chair in some metropolitan symphonic orchestra, rather than somehow, someway verifying her circumstance. To learn she'd been in Nebraska all along and the mother of his child, no less. Oh, yeah. He'd been knocked for a loop. Now that he'd settled into his new reality, his heart's desire was clear.

All I want for Christmas...

Problem was Mason was pretty sure he was on Santa's naughty list. He'd broken more than a few women's hearts, nursed far too many hangovers, disappointed his mom and pissed off his dad—all in the last eight months. His efforts as an off-site representative for RAVI had been half-hearted at best, so that counted as another black mark. Personal discontent was no excuse for shabby professionalism.

When he'd been at the helm, filling his brother's shoes, at least he'd given the job his all. Not his personal dream but it was his personal best. Stepping down had merely given him an excuse to flounder. Several months of wallowing and wondering: *What the hell am I doing with my life?* He'd told Chrissy he was still looking for his dream gig. True. On a dare he'd even applied for his dream gig via an internet site geared to finding people's dream jobs, dream homes, dream vacations... Another half-assed effort on his part. He'd only filled out a third of the data form, if that.

Armed with a loaded shopping bag, Mason paused at the stairwell landing. The girl who'd nudged him into applying at Impossible Dream had been the same girl who'd stood him up at the Mile High Christmas Extravaganza. If not for her, he would've opted for hanging out in the sound booth rather than sitting in the audience. If not for her he wouldn't have been waiting... He wouldn't have seen Melody... Or run into Chrissy.

"Crazy coincidence." *Absolutely.* Still, Mason thought as he continued up the stairs, what if by applying for an impossible dream he'd kick-started some cosmic chain of events? What if being a husband and father was his dream gig?

"You'd be damn good at it, Slick," his brother chimed in from beyond.

Yeah. I would. He knew it as sure as he knew the sun would rise in the morning. As sure as he knew how to ring out microphones, program a digital sound console, and how to replicate and riff off of Hendrix's version of the *Star Spangled Banner.*

If not his dream gig, Mason thought as he entered the bedroom and saw Chrissy snuggled in blankets, marrying and caring for this woman and their child gave him purpose. All he knew was that being here felt right. And being with her felt even better.

Smiling at his approach, Chrissy rubbed her mittened hands together. "I'm starving. Let's see what you have in that mystery bag, Slick."

He stopped cold. "Why did you call me that?"

"What? Slick? I don't know. It just came out. Why?"

"That's what my brother called me."

"Oh. Sorry. Wow." She hugged her knees to her chest. "I swear it just popped out."

Mason shook off a shiver, set his phone and tablet on the nightstand and passed Chrissy the shopping bag. "That's okay." He sat on the edge of the bed, only inches from her, and unlaced his boots. "I swear Jimmy's been in my head all day. Sometimes it feels like he's looking out for me. Sounds crazy, huh?"

"No. Bella, my cousin, says that about her mom. We lost Aunt Laura last year. A shock and a blow to us all, but especially Bella and Uncle Archie."

"What happened, if you don't mind me asking?"

"A stroke. And she was only in her mid-fifties. Just goes to show how unpredictable and fragile life can be," she said as she raided the bag. "One minute you're here—"

"—the next you're gone. A sure-fire reason to live in the moment."

"And to the fullest."

"No wasted opportunities."

"No bullshit."

Mason grinned as their gazes locked. "You always were a straight-shooter. Just one of the things I loved about you."

She flushed. "Here. You uncork the wine," she said, passing him the bottle then nabbing the two crystal goblets he'd found in the cabinet.

"No cork. Screw cap," he said. "More and more wineries are going that route these days." He poured them both a modest serving of merlot.

Chrissy raised her glass in a toast. "To your brother, Jimmy."

"To your Aunt Laura." Mason tapped his fancy goblet to hers, dissolving the lump in his throat with a swallow of wine. "As dinner goes," he said in a lighter tone, "it's not much. I thought it would just be me tonight."

"It's a guy meal, all right," she teased while sorting through his booty. "Pepperoni, crackers, chips, cheese. You'll hit it off great with Zeke. Well, once we get past the introductions anyway."

"I hope so," Mason said, realizing now that if he married Chrissy, he'd be gaining a new brother as well as a wife. In-laws and assorted other relatives. Were they all as down-to-earth as Chrissy? "So your dad and Zeke, they got home okay?"

"Yes, thank you for asking. Windbreaks intact," she said while breaking open the box of crackers. "Cattle safe and accounted for."

Mason divvied out paper plates and cheap napkins. "What's a windbreak?"

"In a nutshell," she said while slicing cheese, "it's a natural or manmade barrier—a shelterbelt of trees, stacked bales of hay or straw, a porous wooden structure. Windbreaks reduce wind speed in a protected zone, reducing severe wind chill. Yes, the cattle have thick hides and grow winter coats that help insulate their bodies from the cold, but that's not always enough for the more mature or newborn animals."

"So by braving that storm, in rebuilding or reinforcing those windbreaks, your dad and brother saved the lives of however many cattle were at risk."

"With the help of Mr. Morgan and a couple of his ranch hands, yes."

"Speaks volumes of your family. Helping out like that. Surely they had concerns of their own."

"Dad's the best at what he does. Our ranch, our livestock were secure. Zeke...he's the best at what he does, too—going head to head with Mother Nature, but he also grew up on a ranch. He loves and respects all varieties of critters. He'd do anything to save even one creature, let alone several."

She frowned and Mason's heart squeezed. "What?"

"I try not to think about it much, but a couple of years ago this region got pummeled by an unseasonal blizzard," she said. "We weren't prepared. Countless heads of cattle perished. It was awful. Horrific, actually. Arlo Morgan was one of the hardest hit. His son, Bryce, bailed him out of a financial catastrophe and now Bryce is facing ruin himself."

"How so?"

"Long story short, he owns and runs The Coyote Club, one of the two bars in town. Although Bryce sank a crap load of money into the joint, it's going down. Only so many people to support local business. He dropped into the bakery today to buy some desserts for his crew. It won't soften the blow when he tells them he's being forced to close his doors—right before Christmas, no less—but it was a sweet gesture. I wouldn't be surprised if Bryce drained the last of his savings to pay his employees some sort of holiday bonus and to compensate the contracted musicians he'll have to cancel. Big-hearted jock."

"Wait," Mason said as something clicked. "Bryce Morgan. Bryce—The Bullet—Morgan?"

"The closest thing Nowhere has to a hometown celebrity," Chrissy said as she sipped more wine. "Although Bella's in the process of making a name for herself. Local librarian turns famous author."

"Your cousin writes books?"

"Fairy tales. Once you get to know her more," Chrissy said with a smile, "you'll totally get it."

"Your friends seem like an interesting bunch," Mason said as they munched on his "guy" meal. The heat from the electric fireplace warmed him nearly as much as Chrissy's company. All that was missing was Melody. And Rush. "I assume this is the same bunch you mentioned five years back. The Inseparables?"

She raised a brow. "Yes, and I mentioned them in passing. That's some memory you've got."

Mason reached over and tucked her soft hair behind her ear. "I remember everything about that week. Every word, every song, every expression, every touch. That's why now, this, us feels so natural. The connection's still there and as strong as ever. At least for me."

"I feel it, too," she said causing his heart to jerk in his chest. "Otherwise I wouldn't be sitting in this bed with you."

"Anything more going to happen in this bed?" Mason couldn't help asking. "Aside from sleeping?"

She drank more wine then met his gaze. "I also remember every word, every song, every expression and every touch. Knowing us and how we roll, I'm guessing *more* is inevitable."

Mason had been fighting a hard-on since the moment he'd walked into Buzz-Bees and spied Chrissy in that fuzzy cap and frilly apron. Now it raged like the storm outside.

She nibbled on cheese, watching him with wary eyes. No doubt she expected him to jump on her seductive assumption—to jump her.

As much as he wanted the sex, he wanted her trust more.

He shifted, trying to ease his sudden discomfort while affecting a casual tone and trying not to obsess on the fact that he might be getting naked with this woman tonight. If not tonight, soon. "So tell me more about your friends."

* * *

"These were great," Mason said, his voice slightly strained. "Thank you for sharing them with me. Do you think," he cleared his throat. "Would you mind emailing me a couple?"

Chrissy tapped into his restrained emotion, her chest aching as she imagined herself in Mason's shoes. What would it feel like to learn, out-of-the-blue, that you had a child in this world? A child who'd experienced four and a half years of special moments and challenges without you?

In going through some of the pictures and videos stored in her tablet, Chrissy relived several Melody "firsts"—first birthday, first walk, first haircut, first pony ride—along with various special or random moments over the years.

Mason had missed them. All of them.

"Here." She passed him her tablet. "You choose."

They were lying in bed, side-by-side, shoulder-to-shoulder. Under the blankets, but fully clothed. Mason had turned out the lights, still the room glowed and flickered with the amber lighting from the artificial fire. The heater provided warmth, but an icy wind seeped through the windows, therefore the room temperature wasn't toasty as much as bearable.

Chrissy snuggled a little closer to Mason, watching as he opened her photo gallery app and clicked on his choices. Rather than a couple, he chose several photos. Most of them featured Mel. Some featured both Chrissy and Mel. Mother and daughter mugging for selfies.

Heart pumping, she watched as Mason emailed himself memories he hadn't been a part of. When showing him the pictures, she'd also shared a few stories, most of them sweet and funny because, yeah, that's how Mel rolled. The kid was a hoot and a blessing.

When he'd asked about Mel's impaired hearing, Chrissy had tensed up, but she'd shared openly. Full disclosure. Since Mason had a background in audio, he easily absorbed the bulk of Melody's limitations and what Chrissy had done in order to advance her education and means of communication. Chrissy especially appreciated that he didn't bombard her with suggestions. Instead of making her feel like she hadn't done enough, he applauded her efforts. She knew without asking that his wheels were turning. And she knew, at some point, he would offer advice.

Amazingly, she didn't mind. In fact, she looked forward to his expertise and input. She'd always had the support of her friends and family, but this was different.

This was Melody's father.

Chrissy tingled with a zap of happy as she placed her tablet on the night stand alongside her phone. "Your turn. Got any pictures of Rush?"

"You want to see pictures of my dog?"

"I think I should know what Mel and I are getting into," she teased, hoping to lighten his spirits.

"Mmm." He reached for his phone and scrolled his glowing screen. "He's a mutt, just so you know. Irish Wolfhound mix. Mix undetermined. And we don't do those frou-frou cuts when we visit the groomer. He's kind of naturally, um, scruffy."

"So he's not a pedigree and he's not pretty." Suppressing a grin, Chrissy wiggled her fingers. "Let me see."

"All right. But you've been warned."

She nabbed the phone and focused on the mutt Mason had adopted from a shelter. Rush was bigger than she'd expected. Taller than a Shepard or Lab. The brown coat of his lean body had been buzzed a little, but his hound face sported lots of scruffy long hair.

"What he lacks in looks, he makes up for in temperament. He's gentle and loyal, smart, yet dopey."

"He's adorable."

"Ya think?" Mason leaned his head closer to hers, muscling in on her pillow and looking up at the screen as she scrolled to the next shot. "That's us after an impromptu tussle in the snow last week."

Chrissy stared up at the motley duo, Mason hugging the

big dog as they mugged for a selfie. She imagined Melody playing with the fun-loving pair and experienced another happy zap. "Can I send these to myself?"

He smiled. "Sure."

While forwarding the photos to her email, she mused on the fact that, though wealthy, Mason lived a modest life. He wasn't one to flaunt his money and he reveled in simpler pleasures. It was refreshing. Somewhat surprising and wholly wonderful. Pensive, she passed back his phone, and then rolled in to face him.

He rolled in as well and after a moment of silence he raised a brow. "You look a little intense."

"Just thinking."

"Intense thoughts."

They were practically nose to nose, their bodies close, so close, but not quite touching. Except for their feet. They both wore thick socks and they'd instinctually rubbed their feet together to generate more warmth. Silly, but the gesture struck Chrissy as intimate. And sweet.

"Just so I'm clear," she said. "We're going to trust this attraction, move forward as a couple."

"You're wary."

"I can't help it. You have to admit it's a little crazy. We come from different worlds. We haven't seen each other in five years and before that we were only together for one week. Also... I know you've never been close with your parents and I know you miss your brother. I worry you're using Mel and me to fill that void in your life. That's a lot of pressure."

He pursed his lips in thought, then nodded. "I've always longed for what I don't have—a warm loving family. So, yeah. You and Mel, the thought of you and Mel and me together, living and loving and making memories, satisfies a deep need. But know this, even if you put the brakes on now, my life is still fuller than ever before. No matter what, you're both in my heart."

Holy... Chrissy closed her eyes, her pulse racing as his words wrapped around her soul—a soothing cocoon, an inspiring nudge. Breathless, she summoned an almighty dose of derring-do. An ocean of boldness and a wisp of faith.

She met his anxious gaze. "I'm not putting on the brakes,

Mason. I'm racing headlong into this crazy scenario—us as a family. I want to try. I want to...sparkle." For Melody.

"Never mind that last part," she said when he furrowed his brow.

He smoothed a hand down her arm. "Anything else?"

"I don't know how to introduce you to Mel," she said honestly. "I can't just say: *This is your daddy*. How would I explain?"

"I've been thinking about that. She's too young for the full-blown story. Maybe it's better to allow our relationship to develop naturally. The more time we spend together—the three of us—the more she sees the affection between you and me, the sooner she'll start thinking of us as a family. And eventually she'll think of me as daddy. When it's time to reveal our past, we'll know."

"That will require a lot of patience on your end."

"Anything worth having is worth waiting for. Although I'm having a hard time with that notion where you're concerned." He leaned closer and pressed his mouth to hers, his tongue teasing the seam of her mouth, coaxing her to open to him.

Chrissy melted in his arms, her mind and body regressing five years. She knew his body intimately, the feel of him, the taste of him. She fantasized about the bare skin and sculptured sinew beneath his thermal pullover. She knew she'd come apart the moment he slid inside. Her entire being tingled in anticipation.

Five years of celibacy hadn't been so bad—until now.

He shifted, moving over her, the weight of his body—so familiar, so good. She wiggled against his erection, slid her fingers beneath the hem of his shirt. His skin was warm, his muscles bunching as she smoothed her hands over his sides and back. She wanted more. She wanted naked. Skin-to-skin.

Meanwhile, he explored her curves through the fabric of her clothes, while kissing her into a frenzied mess of need.

Blood burning, chest heaving, she gasped as he broke the kiss, as he rose to his elbows and dropped his forehead to hers with a groan. "What's wrong?" she asked. "Why did you stop?"

"I want to make love to you in the worst way, Christmas Mooney. Up until about five seconds ago, the dude down south was all for it. But then I had a thought. Last time around we hit it fast and feverish from night one. And it was," he shook his head, smiled, "unbelievably hot. Sexually we know we're a perfect match. This time around there's more at stake and I want you to know I'm in it for the long haul. I want to do this right. And I sure as hell don't want to meet your parents knowing I took advantage of the situation tonight."

Her body still buzzed from the effects of that mind-blowing kiss, and, okay, maybe a little too much wine. Thinking straight was next to impossible, especially when quite possibly the nicest guy on earth was talking all noble and romantic.

He traced a thumb over her cheek. "I can't tell what you're thinking."

"That makes two of us." She struggled to assess the moment. In the past, the sex had been impulsive and wild and not once had they practiced restraint. Mason, especially, was prone to checking his brain at naked. A slave to lust. Chrissy had found his lack of control exciting. Now, wow, who knew restraint could be a turn on?

Settling into this new level of intimacy, Chrissy dragged her fingers through his hair and cradled the back of his head. "Looks like I'm not the only one who's changed."

"I'd like to think I've matured over the years." He smiled into her eyes, and then fell back on the bed. "Turn away."

She blinked.

"You can't expect me to keep staring at that beautiful face and not jump your bones. Mature does not equal monk-like."

Touched and flustered, Chrissy shifted, pulse racing as Mason pulled her body into his—spoon-like—back-to-front. She swallowed hard, cocooned in his possessive embrace. No sex, yet the connection deepened. "Keeping it real?" she asked.

"As real as I can."

Nine

Once upon a tense Tuesday

Chrissy bolted out of Mason's arms as if the bed was on fire.

Slightly disoriented, he pushed up on the pillows. "What the... What's wrong?"

"It's morning."

"Okay."

She pushed up the long sleeve of her slept-in tee, tapped the watch on her wrist. "It's seven-fifteen. I overslept. I'll be late for work." She stood by the nightstand, rumpled and red-faced. "I forgot to plug in my phone. What if Mel called? What if—"

"Hold up. Come here." Sluggish, Mason dragged his hair off of his face as Chrissy rounded the bed. "Give me your phone." He transferred his charger from his phone to hers then reached out and tugged her down beside him. "Breathe."

She shrugged off his touch, nabbed her charging phone and powered on. "Nothing from Bella or Mel. Text from Mrs. W. Delayed opening," she read. "See you at noon."

"That's a good thing. Why are you frowning?"

"I don't know. Yes, I do. I feel...anxious."

"About the meeting with your family?"

"About everything."

Mason shifted so they were sitting side-by-side. Their arms touched and their sock-clad feet dangled next to each other. Regardless, Chrissy felt a million miles away. "Want to talk about it?"

"Not really. But I'm the one who insisted on full disclosure this time so, yeah. Okay. I'll spill." She tucked her messy hair behind her ears and fixed her gaze on her fuzzy yellow socks instead of making eye contact with Mason. "I was dreaming about our week at the Oakley Festival. About the music we made together on stage and off."

Mason remembered well. Whether they were plugged in or playing acoustically, they complimented and inspired one another. His guitar and her fiddle, a kick-ass combination. "Why does that make you anxious? I'm confused, hon. Performing together was a beautiful thing."

"I don't play anymore, Mason. I haven't touched my violin in almost five years. I avoid concerts and dances and I barely tolerate the radio. You still play guitar. You still frequent concerts and clubs. You still find joy in music. I don't."

She could have knocked him over with a feather. When they'd met, music was her life, her passion. He knew she'd traded a career as a concert violinist for motherhood, but he'd assumed she still played for pleasure. A hundred questions crowded his tongue, but all he asked was, "Why?"

She fisted her hands in the bed covers, gaze still averted. "I've been through this with my family and friends. No one has said it outright, but I know they all think I'm nuts. They understand why I forfeited my dream. A career as a concert violinist takes supreme discipline and dedication. Excelling at my art and being a devoted mother were at odds, and I wasn't about to cheat my baby of my full attention. They get that. What they don't understand is my problem with music overall."

Mason bit the inside of his cheek, mulled her words. "I'm a little lost myself."

"The most special moment of my entire being was when the nurse placed my newborn in my arms. A wonderful, bawling, wrinkly, squirming baby." She smiled a little and rubbed her chest. "The feeling, that moment, it's indescribable. But then later, the doctor pronounced my baby deaf and a part of me died. My passion for music turned to contempt. Instead of bringing me joy, it sparked resentment. How could I enjoy something my daughter would never hear?"

Mason's heart hurt for a half a dozen reasons. Instead of pulling Chrissy into his arms, something he didn't sense she'd appreciate right now, he reached over and covered her hand with his own. "I get it."

She chanced his gaze. "Do you?"

"I do. Except, you're thinking about music from your perspective. Your experiences." He dragged a hand over his stubbly jaw. "I could be talking out my ass here, but after our meeting I googled the hell out of deaf children. I wanted to educate myself. I wanted to...help. If I could.

"I ran across this article about a young teen," he hurried on. "A profoundly deaf girl who tried out for cheerleading position and made the squad. She couldn't hear the count offs for the cheers or the stunts, but learned and participated by sight and touch. She couldn't hear the roar of the spectators, but she could see their reactions to the plays on the field. She had spirit, determination and skill and, with the support of her family and teammates, she fully engaged and excelled in what's considered a hearing person's sport."

Chrissy blew out a breath. "You're telling me Melody can appreciate and enjoy musical experiences in her own way. I know. Or at least, I see it now. The Mile High Christmas Extravaganza opened my eyes in that regard. And I know I can count on you to expose Mel to even more audio-based experiences. That means the world to me, Mason. But I need you to know that, although I'll go along with whatever, I can't fully engage myself. Don't expect me to haul my fiddle out of the cedar chest just because you feel like jamming."

Something told him this grudge with music ran even deeper, but she pushed off the bed, signaling an end to the discussion.

"I just want you to be happy, Chrissy. Whatever that entails."

She moved into his arms of her own accord and hugged him hard. "Like father, like daughter."

* * *

Reclaiming pure joy and finding her happy was proving a jumbled affair. Chrissy knew it wouldn't be easy, but she wished ID.com hadn't been so cryptic. Had they sent her the tickets intending to reawaken her love of music or to rekindle her affair with Mason? Was it as simple as seeing and accepting the impact music could have on Melody's life?

Maybe it was all three.

Maybe those tickets were the impetus for owning and controlling one's fate.

Maybe the key to full-blown happy was to trust in the fortitude and tolerance of family and friends.

One thing was certain, the more she expressed her thoughts, her trials and hardships, her challenges and concerns rather than locking them away, the lighter she felt. That thought fueled her eagerness to come clean with her parents and Zeke. About Mason and their past. Not to mention their intended future.

But first she needed to plant a seed with Mel.

The morning was cold, but clear. The plow and salt trucks had done their thing, probably twice by now. The roads were dodgy, but manageable. Joe Savage's place was just down the way and around the corner. Mason insisted on driving. Chrissy didn't argue. Yesterday Mrs. W had likened her to a ball of tightly wound rubber bands. Today she felt one twist from snapping.

"Nice house," Mason said as the renovated Victorian came into view.

"Savage invested a lot of time and money into this property," Chrissy said, while fiddling with her scarf. "It used to be attached to a small amusement park—Rootin' Tootin' Funland. He inherited it from his uncle. Unfortunately, the park suffered a beating. Storms and neglect. He ended up razing it—much to our disappointment. Funland used to be a draw for locals and tourists. A vibrant and viable business. Happy to say he's rebuilding a modernized version closer to town. The grand opening for Wonderland is scheduled for early spring. Good news for Nowhere. Unlike the closure of The Coyote Club."

Mason glanced sideways and Chrissy realized she was

rambling. She'd touched on Funland/Wonderland last night when talking about her friends. But instead of commenting on her bout of nerves, he blew her away.

"What would you say if I told you I was thinking about approaching Bryce Morgan with an investment offer?"

"Why would you do that?"

"Even though I don't have to work, I like to work. I like people and I've spent a good amount of time in various nightclubs and bars. I have the money and I might just have the vision to turn that place around."

"You haven't even seen Coyote's."

"I didn't say it was a done deal. I said I'm thinking about it. Depends on the venue. On Morgan. Figured I'd swing by for a look after we speak with your folks. After that I'll head out to Denver. Most of my stuff is already in boxes. I just need to hire a moving company, tie up some loose business strings, and pack up Rush. I'll be back in time for the Jingles Jamboree. Thursday evening, right?"

"Lease a house that Mel and I already feel comfortable in. Commit to smoothing things over with my family. Save a local business and several jobs. Move mountains to get back here in time so we can take Mel to a holiday function together." Chrissy narrowed her eyes. "Your idea of keeping it real is seriously warped."

"Can't help myself." He furrowed his brow. "Hey, maybe adopting a pair of angel wings during the holiday season is my dream gig."

"What?"

"Never mind." He flexed his fingers on the wheel while rolling through the gated entrance to Bella's new home. "Oh, hell. Okay. I'm officially nervous. I won't be able to communicate with Melody. Not properly."

Chrissy had concerns, too, but that wasn't one of them. She wanted Mel and Mason to hit it off. She was pretty sure they would. Then again things had been going a little too smoothly with this Hallmark-like reunion. Something had to go horribly wrong at some point. Didn't it?

"I'll translate for you," she said, once again placing herself in his shoes. No matter what she was feeling right now, Mason's anxiety had to be two-fold. "I do it all the time in the course of our daily lives. She's used to it. Also Bella and

Georgie are pretty fluent in signing. Savage, not as much, but he gets by." She reached across the seat and squeezed his thigh. "Just be yourself. An angel," she teased.

Mason smirked, but reached over and squeezed her leg as well. "Let's do this," he said, then hopped out and rounded the hood to help her down. The drive was plowed but the drifts were high.

Chrissy glanced at the porch as the front door opened and her cousin stepped out with a bright smile and a welcoming wave. "That's Bella," she told Mason. "You remember her from Denver. And that cat circling her ankles? That's Killer."

"Not for anything, but the big red bow on his collar dilutes the fierceness of the name."

"Bella's doing, I'm sure."

Just then Georgie squeezed into the doorframe and Mason tensed. "They're going to eat me alive."

They'd given him a hard time in Denver, that's for sure. But that was then. Chrissy smiled. "You're wrong." She'd texted them yesterday and again this morning. Angel and Emma, too. They all knew the gist of the scoop. Chrissy nabbed Mason's hand in a show of solidarity and affection as they climbed the stairs. "Hey, guys," she said to her friends. "Thanks so much for taking care of Mel."

"Our pleasure," Georgie said then glanced at Mason and raised a brow. "Welcome to Nowhere, Romeo."

Bella nudged her. "We've got hot coffee and homemade cookies. Come on in." She led them into a toasty living area. Every inch of the room sported some kind of festive decoration.

"Geez, Bella," Chrissy said. "It looks like a holiday factory exploded in here."

"I like it," Mason said, his gaze landing on the six-foot spruce. Not that you could see even one needle, what with all the garland, tinsel, and ornaments.

"Mel helped with the popcorn garland," Bella said. "She's in the dining room right now with Joe. They've been working on a craft. You know those two when it comes to art. My husband's an artist," she said to Mason.

"Former cop. Working artist. The brains behind Wonderland. Chrissy told me."

Chrissy sensed his impatience. She was anxious, too. She

shifted and peeked in the dining room, her heart pounding as she caught sight of her daughter, head down and focused intently on her craft.

Savage saw Chrissy and touched Melody's arm.

Mel looked up and smiled. She bolted from her chair and came barreling into the room.

Chrissy let go of Mason's hand in order to stoop down and brace for her daughter's affectionate assault. Mel practically knocked her flat. Laughing, Chrissy hugged her hard then eased the munchkin to arm's length. She spoke and signed. "Hi, baby. Did you have fun?"

Mel's hands and fingers flew. Her eyes—the same shade of blue as Mason's—danced.

Chrissy responded. "Yes, I saw the popcorn string. Good job! Hey, I brought a friend. Remember this guy?"

Mason dropped to his knees beside her and awkwardly signed, "Hi, Mel," one letter at a time.

Chrissy's heart squeezed. He must've boned up on basic finger spelling.

Mel beamed at him and signed, "Hi." She glanced at Bella.

Bella signed and said, "Yes, this is the man I told you about. Mommy's friend, Mason."

Mel did a one-eighty, ran past Savage giving him a high-five, and zipped back to the dining room table.

Mason's shoulders slumped, but Chrissy knew her daughter well. She knew by the way Mel had smiled at Mason that she liked him. Chrissy squeezed his shoulder and motioned him toward the sofa. By the time they'd shed their coats and sat down, side-by-side, Mel had raced back. She had two homemade ornaments in hand. She passed one to Chrissy.

"So beautiful," Chrissy signed and said. "Thank you, baby."

Then Mel handed a similar ornament to Mason and signed.

Chrissy blew out a breath and put one arm around the emotional man who was staring teary-eyed at his gift. A snowflake cut out of construction paper and accented with green glitter and an "M" made out of red yarn. "She said, Merry Christmas, Mason. This is for your tree."

He smiled at Melody. "Tell her I love it. Tell her I'd love it even more if she'd help hang it on my tree. Tell her I have a dog..."

He whipped out his phone and scrolled to a picture of Rush. He showed the picture to Mel.

Chrissy scrambled to speak his heart. "Mason and Rush are moving here," she told her daughter. "They want us to visit and play."

Mel beamed at the picture of the dog, then beamed at Mason and pumped a happy fist. Then she signed and skipped off.

Chrissy translated. "She wants to make an ornament for Rush."

Mason pressed his thumbs to his moist eyes. "Oh, hell."

Savage stepped in, saving the day two seconds from Chrissy losing it. "Coffee, anyone? Right. I could use a hand, Rivers."

* * *

Emotionally coldcocked, Mason stumbled into his host's kitchen like a zombie.

The man turned and offered a hand in formal greeting. "Joe Savage."

"Mason Rivers.

"You okay?"

"Do I look okay?" Mason braced his hands on his knees, dropped his head. "Damn."

"Bella filled me in. Must be one hell of an adjustment."

"You can say that again." This time when he laid eyes on the little girl with the long blond hair and huge blue eyes, she wasn't just a cute stranger, she was his beautiful daughter.

That smile. So warm and accepting.

Those eyes. Full of intelligence and joy.

As she'd chatted with her mom about popcorn garland, Mason had reflected on the photos Chrissy had shared the night before. Snapshots of Mel's life. A montage of "firsts". He made a mental note to keep it together enough when he got back out there to ask Bella to snap a phone shot of him with Chrissy and Melody. Their first family photo. "Ah, Christ."

"Hang tight."

Rubbing his chest, Mason glanced up as Savage pulled a bottle of liquor from a cupboard.

He poured two fingers of whiskey and passed the glass to Mason. "Mel's a sweet kid. Chrissy... She's a tough nut, but I like her. Lots of people like her. Including the county sheriff, Ryan McClure, who, by the way, is Georgie's half-brother. McClure's also tight with Chrissy's brother, Zeke."

"You going somewhere with this?

Savage leaned back against the counter and folded his arms. "I'm going to put a spin on something McClure said to me after I set my sights on Bella." He cocked his head and regarded Mason with a textbook bad-cop stare. "Hurt Chrissy or Melody and I'll kick your ass."

Mason downed the whiskey in one swallow, knowing he had the meeting with Roger and Zeke Mooney in front of him, remembering his daughter's smile and digging in for the long haul. "Get in line. According to Chrissy, her dad and brother have been primed to bust my butt for years."

Savage smiled—good-cop style. "We're not a bad lot, just a protective one." He nabbed a carafe of coffee, setting it on a tray along with several holiday mugs. "Ready for a second round with your daughter?"

Mason rolled back his shoulders. "Good to go."

"There's a capped snowman tumbler on the top shelf of the fridge. Juice for Mel. Grab that and the tray of cookies."

Encouraged by the man's support, Mason shot "biker dude"—as Chrissy had called him—a grateful look. "Thanks for the save."

"Sure," he said as they moved toward the sights and sounds of holiday cheer. "Just remember the warning."

Ten

"You sure about this?"

"After that hour with my daughter, I can endure anything." Mason parked his SUV behind Zeke's monster wheels. "I can tell you one thing. I promise not to cry when I meet your parents."

Chrissy's lip twitched. Mason had gotten teary with his daughter twice. Although he kept those tears in check, it had been damned sweet all the same. "In order to salvage your pride," she teased, "I pretended not to notice."

"Everyone noticed." He killed the engine and glanced toward the main cabin. "What about you? Braced for your family's reaction?"

"I am." Chrissy tugged her cap lower, then stiffened her spine. "They know I'm bringing a guy over to meet them. They're happy about that, so they're in a good mood. I'm going to spit out the details, roll right over the crappy stuff, and lay out our intentions. I'm focused on the future, Mason. On us. On happy."

He reached across the seat, cupping the back of her neck, and angling in for a kiss. Brief. Tender. Hot. "A kind heart and fierce determination. Some things haven't changed at all." He held her gaze. "I love you, Christmas Joy Mooney."

Her heart pounded and her throat squeezed. Her brain

went on vacation for a day or forty. Time blurred as she fought for a sane thought and word. "I...um..." *Wow*? "Did you have to tell me that right this instant?"

He smiled. "Yeah. I kind of did."

"Are you waiting for me to say it back?"

"I can wait."

"I don't do sappy. I haven't since Napa."

"Okay."

How could he possibly be so nice? So unflappable? So charming? "Damn you, Romeo." She cradled the sides of his face and poured her heart into a kiss. Not so brief. Not so tender. Lava hot.

She eased away and he nodded. "Read you loud and clear, Juliet."

"Let's do this." Primed to get this meeting over, to shed the last of her secrets and to embrace pure joy, Chrissy pushed out of the car, meeting Mason before he got a chance to open her door. She grasped his hand and hurried him toward the rambling log house with the smoking chimney.

The wreath on the front door bounced as the door swung in and Zeke stepped out.

Chrissy smiled. "Hey, Zeke. This is—"

"I know who it is." Instead of offering his hand in greeting, he clipped Mason's jaw with a right hook.

Caught off guard, Mason stumbled back, falling off the porch and landing in a snow drift.

Chrissy gasped or screamed, she wasn't sure, but she definitely gave Zeke hell as she scrambled to help Mason to his feet.

"Dammit, boy." Roger Mooney grabbed his son by the shoulder and jerked him back.

"I thought I'd feel better," Zeke said while shaking out his fist. He grinned at his parents then scowled at Mason. "I do."

Wide-eyed, Eva glanced from Chrissy to Mason and back. "Georgie slipped to Ryan. Ryan called Zeke."

"You've got some explaining to do," Roger said, and then waved them both inside.

The house was warm and inviting. Not so much her family. Chrissy's plan fell apart as she scrambled for words. Any words.

Mason broke the tense silence. "My name is Mason

Rivers, sir." He extended a hand to her father while working his assaulted jaw. "Your daughter and I met five years ago, a whirlwind romance. I'll spare you the details of that week—"

"Smart."

"And tell you simply that I loved her then and I love her now."

"What the hell happened in between?" Zeke blasted.

"I didn't know about Melody. There was a miscommunication. I don't have that part figured out yet. But I swear to you, if I had known I had a child, I would have offered my full support."

"But if you loved one another," Eva asked Chrissy, "why did you split up in the first place. Why keep the relationship secret? You could have at least told us his name."

"She was afraid if you knew my name, you'd track me down," Mason said.

"She's right about that," Roger said with an enigmatic glance at his daughter.

"Someone intercepted Chrissy's email, an email meant for me, and shared the news of her pregnancy with my father. Who in turn instructed his lawyer, our family lawyer, to write a cease and desist letter of sorts to Chrissy. That letter made threats pertaining to your family's financial ruin should she ever contact our family again." Mason rolled back his shoulders then took her hand. "That's why your daughter withheld my identity and forged ahead as a single mother. She was protecting you and Melody."

"Son of a bitch," Zeke said.

"Where's the letter?" Roger asked.

"I burned it," Chrissy said. Her first words. Words that caused a universal frown.

Her dad shifted, a six-foot-four mountain of frustration and anger. He jerked his head toward Mason but addressed Chrissy. "How am I supposed to confront his asshole father with no proof of threat?"

She swallowed hard. "I don't want you to confront Boyd Rivers. I want you to accept Mason and the fact that we want to move forward as a couple."

"You haven't seen each other in five years!" Zeke exploded.

Eva shushed her son. "Seems we have a lot to sort out. I

have coffee brewing on the stove. Give me a hand, Christmas."

Roger elbowed Zeke. "Grab a bottle of whisky. You." He pointed at Mason. "Take a seat."

Mason squeezed Chrissy's hand before she finally let go and followed her mom into the kitchen. It smelled like toast and coffee and goodness. Tears stung her eyes as her mom grasped her shoulders.

"I have two questions. Do you love him?"

"With all my heart. I know it seems crazy, but—"

"Is he a good man?"

Chrissy crooked a wobbly smile. "Too good to be true. He's already bonded with Mel. He's moving here and—"

"That's all I need to know." Eva hugged her tight and smiled against Chrissy's cheek. "Now. Let's go side up with Mason and do battle with your dad and Zeke."

Eleven

Once upon a special night
One week later

"Sorry I'm late!" Chrissy rushed into Café Caboose, her purse and a shopping bag looped over her arm. Winded, she plopped into the vacant seat next to Emma. "Did you order yet?"

Emma nodded. "Choo-Choo Cheeseburgers all around. Extra fries for you as specified by you."

"Awesome. Thanks." She swiped off her cap and smiled at her friends. Emma, Angel, Georgie, Bella. All the Inseparables, minus their gentle, secretive east-coast transplant. Chrissy was so thrilled to be with all of them, she didn't even mind the holiday music playing loudly in the background. 'Twas the night before Christmas Eve. Of course, the staff at Caboose were cranking up the jolly.

"Talk about miracles," Chrissy said in all sincerity. "Between everyone's manic schedules, I was beginning to think we'd miss our traditional dinner this week."

"I wasn't worried for a minute," Bella said.

"That's because you're obscenely optimistic," Emma said. "As it was, I was the only one who had every night open for the last six days—surprising and somewhat depressing. I thought I had a life. Now I'm wondering. Even with three jobs, I have much more time on my hands than any of you.

"You," she said to Bella, "had conflicts with the library and that kids' function with Savage. Angel's neck deep in her charity work. Georgie had commitments with her assorted half and step siblings. Chrissy, well, we all know what she's been up to," Emma finished with a wink.

Chrissy flushed.

Angel smiled. "I think it's sweet. And inspiring. Reunited with her true love. The father of her child. Five years of separation and now they're making up for lost time by spending as much time together as possible."

"You can't blame Chrissy for being joined at the hip with Mason," Georgie said. "The man's not only handsome and charismatic, he's also a mover and shaker. Angel was desperate to sell her house on Eagle Butte. He's buying it. Bryce was three days from shutting down Coyote's. Mason swooped in and saved the day. Within a week and a half, the man landed a home, a business, wooed back his love, won over his daughter, and...he's pretty much charmed the whole of Nowhere, including Chrissy's family." Georgie frowned and blushed. "No thanks to my loose lips."

"Would you let that go?" Chrissy said as she motioned the waitress for a coffee. "If I was going to be mad at anyone, it would be Ryan. He's the one who tipped off Zeke. Hard to be mad though, when I know his intentions were good. For years I gave Ryan the impression Mason was a bastard, so naturally he was worried."

"Yeah," Georgie said, "but because of me and Ryan, Zeke punched Mason."

"And Mason took it like a champ," Chrissy said, smiling a little when she remembered how he'd stayed true to his word. He'd focused on smoothing things over with her family. Slow going, but it was going. His developing relationship with Mel, on the other hand, was moving at lightning speed. Chrissy wasn't sure who her daughter adored more: Mason or his dog.

"All I know," Emma said as the waitress served their burgers, "is that at the rate you two are going, you'll be married by the New Year."

"I doubt that," Chrissy said, focusing on her fries rather than her friends. "We haven't even..."

"What?" Georgie asked.

"You're kidding!" Emma said.

Chrissy shushed her, feeling as red as the ketchup she squirted onto her plate.

"You've been hot and heavy for over a week," Emma said in an excited whisper. "Considering the heat level of the public affection, I just assumed you were burning up the sheets at home."

Angel gawked. "You mean you haven't... Wow. That's a stunner."

"Color me surprised," Georgie said.

"I know you said Mason wanted to take it slower this time," Bella said, "but, I'm with Georgie. Every time you two are in the same room, the windows steam up. I just assumed..."

"What are you waiting for?" Angel asked.

"It's not me. It's him. Every time we get close, he puts on the brakes. It's like all of a sudden he's gone all old-fashioned on me."

"When you put it like that," Bella said, as she dressed her burger, "it's sort of sweet. Definitely romantic."

"Try frustrating." Chrissy stuffed a handful of fries into her mouth. She'd been eating a lot lately. *Oral compensation for the lack of sex.* "It's been five years since..."

Angel angled her head. "Since you and Mason..."

"Since me and anyone," Chrissy blurted then lowered her voice, "did it."

"Five years of celibacy?" Georgie asked wide-eyed.

"That's just wrong," Emma said with a headshake.

"What? You thought I was sleeping around?" Chrissy asked Georgie.

"Of course, not. But I assumed you'd, you know," she said with a furtive glance around, "done some horizontal barn-dancing with someone at some point. How would I know? You're always so private about that stuff."

"If you want to, um, mambo so badly," Angel said. "Why don't you make it impossible for him to say no?"

Chrissy raised a curious brow.

"Wow," Emma said. "It has been a long time. Be the aggressor. Seduce him. Wear something hot—"

"Or nothing at all," Georgie said with an ornery grin.

"Joe likes it when I dress up in costume," Bella said,

causing everyone to pause mid-chew. "Drives him senseless."

"So, so wrong," Emma said.

"What?" Bella asked, then snorted and rolled her eyes. "Not my princess gown or any of the other stuff I wear for storytelling with the kids. I'm talking sexy stuff. You know," she said with a wiggle of her fair brows. "Nurse Goodbody, Friendly Skies Flight Attendant, Deputy Patdown."

Angel buried her red face in her hands. "TMI."

"Holy crow," Georgie said.

"Who knew you had it in you?" Emma asked then looked to Chrissy and jerked a thumb at Bella. "That's what I'm talking about."

"I get it," Chrissy said. If her goody-two-shoes cousin could seduce biker dude senseless, surely Chrissy could obliterate Mason's restraint. "I don't do sappy, but I can do sexy."

"Where's Mason right now?" Bella asked as she slurped egg nog.

"At his house." Although, Chrissy and Melody had been spending so much time there with him and Rush it was beginning to feel like *their* house.

"Where's Melody?" Georgie asked.

"With mom and dad. Baking cookies and helping to prepare for Christmas Eve."

"Then what are you doing here?" Emma asked.

"Mason all alone in that big house," Bella said.

"Timing is everything," Angel said. "Well, timing and attitude."

Chrissy blinked at her friends. "But we haven't even exchanged our gifts."

"We can amend that," Emma said.

On cue, everyone dipped into their shopping bags, checking name tags and passing beautifully wrapped packages to the appropriate Inseparable.

"Whatever it is," Bella said as they all traded gifts. "I love it."

"You shouldn't have," Georgie said to everyone even though she didn't know the contents of her packages, "But thank you!"

"What a surprise!" Angel said. "Or at least it will be."

"You can open these later," Emma said to Chrissy while

reloading her gift bag.

Georgie shoved aside Chrissy's half-eaten meal. "Dessert's waiting at home."

Somewhat stunned, but inspired, Chrissy looped her scarf around her neck. Her pulse raced as her mind mentally scoured her lingerie drawer. Nabbing her coat and bag, she stood and smiled at her friends. "You're the best."

They smiled back and answered as one. "We know."

* * *

"To wrap or not to wrap? Do I do the friend-of-mommy thing or the daddy-Santa thing?"

Rush cocked his head at his person.

Mason cocked a brow at his dog. "You're no help."

Hands on hips, he shifted his gaze from the scruffy mutt to his messy bed, a bed overflowing with gifts for his daughter. Chrissy had asked him not to go overboard. "So much for keeping it real."

The doorbell rang.

Instead of barking, Rush nudged Mason's hand. A new skill he'd learned in order to alert Melody of a sound. Rush would never be a full-fledged, top-notch hearing dog, but he was coming along with some basics.

Everything, relating to their move to Nowhere, was coming along and coming together in a calm and grounded manner, Mason thought as he loped down the stairs. Even though he'd jumped on buying this house and investing in the Coyote Club, it had merely been the groundwork to rooting himself in Chrissy's hometown. To dig in with her and her family. To provide a stable home for Melody. Building trust, deepening bonds, nurturing a successful business...that would take time.

"Anything worth having is worth waiting for, working for."

At long last a sense of contentment and purpose fueled his days. Every morning he woke inspired. Every night he counted his blessings. Chrissy and Mel topped the list. He'd never felt more loved in his life.

He swung open the door expecting a delivery man. He'd been receiving packages for several days. His heart slammed against his ribs. "Dad."

"Son."

Mason stood poleaxed. They hadn't spoken since the blowout. He'd had two tense calls from his mother, ordering him to stop this nonsense and come home. He'd ignored her third call.

Wearing a cashmere coat and an enigmatic expression, Boyd shifted his sizable body, snow crunching beneath his boots. "Are you going to invite me in or are we going to have this discussion on your porch?"

Rush sat at Mason's side. He wasn't growling, but his tail wasn't thumping either. Curious, yet cautious. Like owner, like dog.

It was cold and dark and, even though his closest neighbor was a half-mile away, Mason had no interest in airing his dirty laundry in a plain view. He and Chrissy were a lot alike when it came to guarding their privacy. Spine stiff, mood edgy, Mason sent Rush packing then stepped back, allowing the old man to invade his new home.

He led him into the living room without offering to take his coat. A silent signal to state his case and be gone. It wasn't like Mason to be bitter, but dammit he was. Boyd Rivers had robbed him of five precious years and now he was tainting his cherished sanctuary.

A fire crackled in the hearth. The massive Christmas tree twinkled with lights and ornaments, several handmade by Mel. A holiday movie played out on the big-ass plasma screen, featuring the velvety voice of Bing Crosby. Rush had curled up on his bed with a stuffed animal—another gift from Mel.

"Are you alone?" Boyd asked as his grey gaze skimmed the cozy room.

"At the moment."

"I thought maybe..." He worked his jaw then swung a festive shopping bag at Mason. "This is for Melody."

Mason stared at the bag. "You brought my daughter a gift?"

"I was hoping to meet her and...Take the damned bag, Mason. It won't bite."

Heart thudding he relieved his father of the metallic green bag and set it next to the tree.

Boyd stuffed his big hands in his coat pockets. "I was hoping to meet Melody and I wanted to apologize to Miss Mooney. And you. It took a lot of digging, but you were right. There was a letter. A threatening letter and it was sent via Edward's office."

Mason balled his fists at his sides. "But you didn't write it. Or sanction it."

"I did not."

"Then who? Oh, hell." Mason's gut cramped. "Mom?"

"I'm not here to defend or explain her actions. I can't. Not wholly. She's yet to come clean with me on this."

"Why isn't she here? Coming clean with me? What the... So she hired someone to hack into my email? To screen my correspondences? What the hell?"

"Something snapped inside your mom when Jimmy died."

"We all snapped, Dad."

"I've tried to shield you, everyone, from some of her greater...issues. And yes, I've urged her to seek professional help. That's yet to happen." He blew out a breath. "I know she thought you were wild back then. More wild than your brother. She worried you might end up in trouble. I think she saw that email from Miss Mooney as trouble. Saw it as a threat. She was worried about losing you."

"She has lost me." Mason's heart felt like a freaking block of ice. "Because of her selfish manipulation, Chrissy spent almost five years raising Melody as a single parent. Five years of thinking I didn't love her. Five years of thinking I'd rejected our daughter." Frustrated, he shoved his hands through his hair. "Oh, what the hell do you care?"

"I care."

The same words Mason had said to Chrissy during their frazzled reunion.

"I'm a driven man, Mason, and not a particularly warm one. But I care. This isn't easy for me to say, but I'm sorry for forcing you into Jimmy's shoes. I don't think I ever realized how fully miserable you were. But I do know how hard you tried."

Mason stood strong, even though his knees felt like buckling.

Boyd took another look around the room. "You have a

nice place here. I know you're settling in and going your own way, but you'll always be a part of RAVI. If you ever want to take an active role again—just say the word. I wish you and your Chrissy well and I hope to meet that granddaughter of mine sometime soon."

Bing Crosby continued to croon as Mason continued to stare.

His dad glanced at the tree, the tinsel, the lights, Mel's popcorn garland and snowflake ornaments. "I should go. Driver's waiting to take me back to the airport. I couldn't let Christmas go by without seeing you, Mason. As for your mother... I'm hoping that'll work itself out."

He turned to leave.

"I'll show you out."

"I can find my way."

Mason didn't argue. And he didn't have it in him to go all warm and fuzzy on a man who'd never showed an ounce of true affection. Until now. If booking a charter plane to fly across the state to deliver a gift and an apology counted as affection.

"Ah, hell." Mason hurried across the room, Rush trotting behind, tail wagging. He caught up just as his old man's boots hit the porch. "Dad. Thanks for... Merry Christmas."

Boyd turned, nodded. "You don't have to tell her it's from me, but I'd be obliged if you gave that gift to my granddaughter."

Mason nodded, watching as his father strode through the dark to his rented ride. When the car backed out, Mason closed the door and palmed the wall. He looked down at Rush. "Yeah, I know. The season of goodwill. Forgiveness, understanding, and all that. Gonna need some time on this one, Champ." He pushed off the wall. "Time and probably a drink or two."

As they moved back into the living room, Mason's gaze fell on the metallic bag. He wasn't sure how Chrissy would feel about giving Mel a gift from his dad, a man she'd lived in fear of for the last few years.

Only Boyd Rivers hadn't really been to blame.

Curious, Mason stooped down next to the bag. What did Boyd know about little girls? Had he bought a gender appropriate gift? An age appropriate gift? When Mason had confronted his dad about Melody's existence, he'd mentioned she'd been born deaf. Had the old man bought an appropriate gift period?

Mason glanced at Rush who whined.

"I'm with you," he said. "Let's find out."

Mason pulled crinkled red tissue from the bag until his fingers connected with the gift. "I'll be damned."

A small tambourine rigged with multi-colored LED lights. A rhythmic instrument that she could shake or smack like a drum. A musical instrument that flashed and twinkled with a bonus light show.

"Perfect."

Almost as perfect as the card with the handwritten message: *For Melody. March to the beat of your own drum.*

Twelve

Chrissy's knees knocked as she rang the doorbell. She wasn't sure if it was because she was nervous or cold. Probably both. The door swung open and Mason looked stunned. She hadn't called ahead, still.

Weird.

"Sorry," he said. "I thought you were... Never mind." He nabbed her arm and pulled her in out of the cold. "You're not going to believe the night I've had."

"Nothing compared to what's ahead." Before she lost her nerve, she shrugged out of her coat, shivering as it slid down her goose-pimply skin and dropped to her ankles.

"Whoa. What the..." Smiling and palming his forehead, Mason backed into the living room as Chrissy advanced in her knee-high leather boots with the three-inch heels. "Uh, go lie down, Rush."

The dopey-eyed dog curled back in his bed and Chrissy stopped and posed, hands on hips. "Decided to give you your Christmas present a little early."

"You? Naked?

"Naked me is a bonus. The scarf is the gift." The only thing she was wearing aside from the boots. "Made it myself," she said as she seductively slid the long, red cable-knit scarf from her shoulders then hooked it around his neck and reeled him in.

"Beautiful," he said, though his eyes were on her breasts, not the scarf. He cleared his throat, met her gaze. "Thank you."

"My pleasure." She smiled a little, unbuttoning his shirt. "Speaking of my pleasure..."

"Chrissy?"

She pressed seductive kisses to his chest while pushing his shirt off his shoulders.

"What are you doing?"

"If I have to tell you then I'm doing it wrong."

"Let me rephrase."

"You talk too much." She grasped the ends of the scarf and yanked him into a deep kiss, her bare breasts skimming his warm torso. Skin-on-skin.

His hands smoothed down her back and cupped her bottom while she made quick work of his belt.

She slid her hand in his briefs, wrapping her fingers around his...

"Cold. Damn."

"Sorry." Of course her fingers were icy. Sexy had meant no mittens. Self-conscious now, she dropped her forehead to his chest. "Are we ever going to make love?"

Mason threaded his fingers through her hair, cradled the back of her neck. "Please tell me you know I've been dying to be inside you. I was trying to hold out, to move slower, to do things differently than before."

She struck his chest with a half-hearted punch. "Screw that. Nothing was wrong with before. Before was wonderful. Magical. Just not the perfect time. Now's the perfect time. Timing is everything. Timing and attitude."

Mason kissed the top of her head. "You have me there, babe."

He swept her off her feet. Scooped her into his arms and strode toward the stairway.

Now it was her turn to ask, "What are you doing?"

"Taking you to bed. Where's Mel?"

"With Mom and Dad. All night."

"Good." He swept her up the stairs, into the master bedroom. "Ah, dammit."

"What?" She lifted her head from his shoulder and

immediately saw the trouble. A multitude of toys and little clothes crowding up his bed. "Please tell me that's not all for Mel."

"Can we argue about it tomorrow?" he asked as he set her to her feet.

Her lip twitched. "Sure." *So this was sex with a kid in the mix*, she thought as they both cleared the bed. *Different, but just as exciting.*

She activated the electric fireplace as he shucked his jeans. They jumped into bed at the same time. "I love you, Mason Rivers."

He froze. "Did you have to tell me that right this instant?"

She smiled. "Yeah. I kind of did."

"Happy to hear it," he said, gaze soft with emotion. "But it muddles the balls-out sex thing with the heart-pounding romantic thing."

"Mason."

"Yeah?"

"Right this minute? Go with the balls-out sex."

"Right. Thanks. In that case, leave on your boots."

"Only if you wear your scarf."

Grinning, he pushed her back on bed and crawled up her body, all predator-like. The hand-knitted scarf hung from his neck, tickling her skin as he kissed a racy path up her torso then lingered at her breasts.

She moaned with rapture, combing her fingers through his shaggy hair, relishing the weight of his body, the feel of his mouth.

"You taste even better than you smell," he said while nuzzling his neck.

"I'm all for foreplay," she said, throat tight, body tense. "But I'm dying here, Mason. It's been so long. Since you."

He stilled. Pushed up to his elbows and gazed down at her face. "I thought you didn't do sappy."

"Was that sappy?"

"Yeah. It kind of was. And hot. I'm hard as a rock."

"I wouldn't know. That's code, by the way, for: I want you inside me. Now."

He rolled away and she closed her eyes in frustration. But then she heard a drawer open, a package tearing.

Protection.

Before she could blink, he was on top of her, filling her, and, oh... "So good."

"Just like before." He worshiped her body with his hands while rocking against her, and kissing her into a sensual stupor.

"Only better." Her stomach coiled and her heart pounded as she absorbed the intensity of Mason's love. Body trembling with a fast and fierce orgasm, she held tight as he followed her lead. "Heaven."

* * *

She hurried him through foreplay, so he indulged in after-play. Which led to a second round of lovemaking. A little intense and a lot wild. Mason was spent. He was also inspired.

He offered her one of his t-shirts, pajama bottoms, and a pair of thick socks. He dressed in kind then led her downstairs and made them spiked hot cider. She looked damned adorable wearing his gear, curled up on the sofa, drinking holiday cheer.

Rush snored in his bed.

Fire flickered in the hearth.

Lights twinkled on the tree.

Miracle on 34th Street, one of his favorites, showed on the plasma.

Everything was damn near perfect.

Just do it, Slick.

"I really do love my scarf."

She looked from the TV to him and smiled. "I'm glad. It's not much but—"

"You made it, so it's special."

"Don't hate me but your other scarf was kind of hideous."

"You mean festive."

She raised a brow.

He smiled. "Since you gave me my gift early, I'm inspired to do the same."

"You only got me one, right? We agreed and I saw how you buckled with Mel."

"One gift." He pushed off the sofa and plucked her present from beneath the tree. "I hope you like it."

"I'm sure I'll love it." She opened the slightly oversized box and tore through crumpled tissue to get to the smaller jeweler's box. "Oh."

Mason's lungs squeezed as she flipped open the velvety lid. "It's not much. That is, I tried not to go overboard."

She stared at the ring—a modest heart-shaped diamond on a platinum band. "It's beautiful, Mason. It's..." She met his anxious gaze. "Yes."

He laughed, thrilled and relieved. "I didn't even ask yet."

"Oh. Sorry. I—"

He smoothed her hair from her face. "Will you marry me Christmas Joy Mooney? Will you let me love and care for you and our daughter?"

"Yes. Yes, yes, and yes." She rubbed her chest while admiring the ring. "Mel will be so happy."

Mason wasn't sure why, but her words, her body language gave him pause. "What about you, hon? Are you happy?"

"What? Yes. Yes, of course. I...I'm just a little rattled. I..."

Mason took the jeweler's box from her trembling hands and set it aside. "Talk to me."

And still she rubbed her chest.

"Full disclosure," he reminded her.

"Right. Okay. Just know I don't expect you to understand. It's...nonsensical."

Mason pulled her into his side, offering encouragement. "I'm all ears."

She took a deep breath then spewed. "Last month Mel wrote a letter to Santa. She didn't ask for a toy for herself. She asked for a present for her mommy. Quote: *She's always sad even when she's smiling. Instead of making her a toy, can your elves make her happy?*"

"Whoa."

"Yeah. My mom called it a tear jerker then pointed out the obvious. It's up to me, not Santa, to connect with that feeling of pure joy. I don't know how to describe it. The sensation. The state."

"I'm guessing it's close to euphoric. Feeling content and inspired. Happy on steroids."

She angled her head. "Something like that, yes. Mom said I used to sparkle with it."

Mason reflected on the Chrissy he'd known five years

back. Focused, fun, *carefree*. Her edgy effervescence had been unique. On the other hand, when he met her in Denver she radiated with subdued frustration. She'd lightened up since then, but he wouldn't call her carefree. He also remembered something she'd said when they'd touched on moving forward as couple. "*I want to try. I want to sparkle.*"

A concern burrowed into his brain. One he tried to ignore.

"I hated knowing that my daughter was picking up on my inner struggle," Chrissy hurried on. "I thought I'd adjusted pretty well to my life as a single mom. My life as a baker and knitter. It's not like I don't enjoy both. At the very least, I thought I was a positive force in Mel's life. Reading her letter, I felt a little desperate, so I applied to an Internet site that grants impossible dreams. I applied for happy. How crazy is that?"

Mason shifted. "Wait. What?"

"I told you it was nonsensical. In reply, ID-dot-com sent me four tickets to the Mile High Christmas Extravaganza which led me to you and thereafter several random zaps of happy."

Mason listened as Chrissy rambled at breakneck speed, citing specific moments where she'd sparkled for a fleeting moment. He juggled knowing that he'd had his own brush with Impossible Dream and learning how desperate Chrissy was to reconnect with "pure joy".

Two things became clear.

One: She was in deep denial regarding the impact the lack of music had on her life.

Two: She'd do anything to create the illusion of happy for Melody. Including snapping up his marriage proposal without due thought.

The latter was a particular blow to his heart.

"Every time I think I've achieved pure joy, it fades. I wanted forever, Mason. I wanted what I had before... Before..."

"What?"

"Oh, God." She buried her face in her hands.

"Before Melody?"

She spoke over heart-wrenching sobs. "I don't regret her for a minute. Not one second. I just wish..."

Swallowing the painful lump in his throat, Mason scrambled to voice her thoughts. Something associated with guilt. Something massive. "You wish having her hadn't meant giving up your musical aspirations?"

"I wish she hadn't...hadn't been born deaf."

His heart hammered against his ribs as he hugged her, affording what little comfort he could. Forfeiting her musical career wasn't at the root of her misery. No, it was something far deeper.

Mason thought hard before speaking. He knew Chrissy well enough to know she didn't love Mel any less just because she couldn't hear. "You blame yourself. Or is it me? Do you blame me?"

She didn't answer and his mind raced, mentally reviewing some of the research he'd done over the last couple of weeks. "Is it genetic?" This isn't something they'd talked about in depth yet. She'd said the doctors had been unclear regarding the cause of Mel's birth defect. Mason had been wary about pressing too hard, too fast for more information. He'd been taking everything slow, trying not to scare Chrissy off. He'd wondered though.

"There's no history of deafness in my family," he said carefully. "What about yours?"

"No. No history," she croaked. "And I don't blame you, Mason."

"Yourself then. Were there complications during pregnancy? Were you ill? Taking medication?"

"No. Nothing like that, but I... Oh, God. It's too awful to say."

Chest tight, Mason shifted so they were facing each other. He pulled her hands from her red and tear-soaked face. "Whatever it is, it's been festering inside you for almost five years, poisoning your soul. Spit it out."

She nodded and hiccupped over a sob. "There were times during the pregnancy, moments of depression, when I felt lost and scared. I no longer had a grip on my dream or my future. I resented the uncertainty. I felt guilty knowing I'd skipped school for that week. Because of our affair, I'd flushed away all the hard-earned money my parents had invested in my education and training. And, yes, at times I felt bitter knowing I'd pretty much botched any hope of ever being a professional concert violinist. Once my baby was born, things would never be the same. And then she was born and..."

"The doctors pronounced her deaf. And you thought, what? That that was your punishment for resenting uncertainty? For having bitter thoughts? Oh, honey."

"It could have been anything, Mason. Any one of a hundred defects. Why deafness? Why—"

"I don't know. But I do know that it wasn't some sort of Karmic payback for being human. I don't believe for one moment that God punished you, or Mel, for having what you perceive as selfish, bitter thoughts."

He dragged a hand down his face, grappling for calm and concise thoughts. "You need to accept and acknowledge that Mel isn't suffering. She's unique. She's unbelievably happy and loved."

He thought about the LED tambourine in the bag under the tree. "She'll march to the beat of her own drum and she'll be, she is, awesome. You need to believe in Mel's ability to shine in this world exactly as she is," he said while framing Chrissy's sweet, tortured face. "You need to let go of what's dampening your own sparkle. If you can't do that, promise me you'll be open to speaking with a professional who can help."

She swiped at her tears, nodded.

"One last thing," Mason said as his heart bled. "I need you to think hard on why you want to marry me. I can't make you sparkle, Christmas. And you can't count on Santa or his elves or some whimsical matchmaking site. Pure joy? That's on you, babe."

Thirteen

Once upon a Christmas Birthday

Chrissy slept on Mason's question for two nights. Mostly because he suggested they wait until after the holiday to revisit the topic of marriage. Partly because she needed the time to acclimate to the lightening of her soul.

She hadn't realized how severely she'd twisted up and stuffed down a cesspool of toxic emotions until she'd gutted herself for Mason. She'd spent the majority of the last five years directing that internal ugliness toward him and his family.

When she learned Mason hadn't truly turned his back on her and their baby, when he assured her she had nothing to fear from his family, all that negative energy swirled and settled within.

Sharing her deepest, darkest thoughts with Mason had been cathartic. She wasn't dancing on air, but she wasn't drowning in that cesspool anymore either. Just now a playlist of holiday classics blasted from the iPod Zeke had bought for their parents and Chrissy didn't wince once. She even found herself humming along to Silver Bells as her dad and Mason cleaned up the last of the wrinkled and discarded wrapping paper—evidence of a very merry Christmas morning at the Mooneys'.

Later today, she'd enjoy a quiet birthday celebration at Mason's house while Mel opened the gazillion gifts still waiting for her under Mason's tree. So far he'd only gifted his daughter with three things. A stuffed dog from Rush. Pink fuzzy boots from him. And a tambourine that lit up from his dad. He'd only given Mel that gift after he'd told Chrissy the story about Boyd's visit and she'd given her approval. Of course she approved. At this point, and especially knowing Mason's level of angst regarding his mom, Chrissy actually felt sorry for the highly dysfunctional Rivers family.

As for Mel, she swore she was going to wear her fuzzy pink boots every day, even in the summer. She named her stuffed blue dog, Rush 2. And she loved that tambourine. The way the colorful lights flashed and twinkled. The way it felt when she shook and thwacked it. It made Chrissy smile. It made everyone smile. Including Mason who hadn't been fully himself since the night he'd proposed.

He'd gone all out on Christmas Eve, decking the halls with her family. He'd taken a million pictures. He'd kept conversation light and hadn't withheld a smidgeon of affection from Chrissy, even though she knew he was hurting.

He'd once told her most women were more interested in his wallet than him. He knew Chrissy wasn't seduced by his fortune, but he did wonder about her motivations. Just as she worried he expected her and Mel to fill a void, he worried she expected him to free her chained and tarnished "happy".

"You're awfully deep in thought."

Chrissy looked up from the cookie tray she was replenishing and locked eyes with her mom. "Thinking about how lucky I am."

Eva glanced toward the active living room, noted Mason tussling with Mel and Rush, and smiled. "A few minutes ago, Melody cornered me in the kitchen and asked me to write another letter for her." She pulled the noted from her cardigan pocket. "Want a peek?"

Swallowing hard, Chrissy opened the note and read.

"Dear Santa. Mason is the best present ever! Thank you for making mommy smile. And thank you for Rush. We love them. Your forever friend, Melody."

It took a second to catch her breath, but then Chrissy

passed the note back to her mom. "I need to run over to my place for a sec," she said, skirting the dining room table and heading toward the kitchen. "I'll use the back door. Be right back."

"But you're not wearing a coat!"

Chrissy barely heard her mom as she rushed through the kitchen and barreled outside. She barely felt the bite of the freezing air as she tramped through snow then down the shoveled walk that led to her small cabin. The only home she and Mel had ever known until they'd started making a new home with Mason on Eagle Butte Road.

She sailed through the tiny kitchen, through the living room, and into her bedroom, stopping short at the cedar chest containing a few cherished belongings. Heart in throat, she opened the lid and stared down at the black case she'd carried to and from private lessons, to and from university classes, rehearsals, and stages.

With trembling hands she pulled the case from the chest and laid it lovingly on her bed. She opened that lid, too and, for a moment, just stared at the instrument that had essentially been an extension of her for most of her life.

"Long time, no see, my friend."

Swallowing hard, she skimmed her fingers down the violin.

Scroll, pegs, neck, strings, fingerboard, bridge, F-holes, chinrest.

Her pulse skittered and skipped as she primed the bow with rosin then tuned the strings. All by rote.

"You're rusty. I'm rusty. Forgive me if I skip extensive foreplay and get to the main event."

A song whispered through her mind as she readied to play. She closed her eyes, breathed, and put bow to strings. It wasn't beautiful, but it was music. It filled her with melancholy for years wasted and joy for the years to come.

She focused on joy.

She sat on the edge of the bed, pouring her heart into a stilted version of *Have Yourself a Merry Little Christmas*. By the time she reached the bridge, she didn't feel so rusty.

When she reached the end of the song, she opened her eyes and saw her mom standing in the doorway, eyes shining with tears.

107

"I was worried about you," she said, "so I ran over to...and then I heard..." She beamed. "You're sparkling."

And tingling, Chrissy thought. *Head to toe. Heart and soul.* "Didn't sound great, but it felt wonderful."

"Sounded beautiful to me. And you... Oh, honey." Eva clasped her hands to her heart. "The old you."

"Only different." Her dream had shifted, along with her passion and priorities.

Not impossible.

Probable.

Doable.

Derring-doable.

"Now if we can just get the light back into Mason's eyes," Eva said. "For all the merry he's making, he seems sad. I don't know what happened between you two but—"

"I'm going to fix it, Mom."

These last two weeks Mason had been the solid force in their lives. So confident. So determined.

"All we need is for one thing to go right. Us."

Chrissy returned her violin to its case. "Could you...Would you please keep this, my playing, to yourself for a while?"

"It won't be easy, but sure."

"And let Mason and Mel know I'd like to get a jump start on my birthday celebration?"

Eva smiled then pushed off and headed out.

Chrissy pulled her phone from her hoodie pocket and made a call. "Hey, Bryce. It's Chrissy Mooney. You know that 'tis-the-season miracle thing?"

* * *

Mason knew Chrissy was up to something, but he couldn't guess what. Saying they'd swing back later for Rush, she hustled him and Mel out of her parents' house and insisted on taking a detour to the Coyote Club.

She refused to say why.

Driving through Nowhere was an eerie affair. The streets were deserted but every storefront and streetlamp boasted festive decorations—a ghost town alive with the spirit of Christmas.

Mason held silent as they rolled down Frontier, his mind

chewing on his splintered mood.

Part of him gloried in the Mooneys' old-fashioned ways—the Christmas Eve dinner, the lazy morning gift-exchange. Like any kid, Mel had been crazy excited about her booty. He'd probably taken a hundred pictures with his phone. Photographic evidence of their first Christmas as a family. That part of him was ecstatic.

Another part feared he'd left reality in the dust when he'd reunited with Chrissy, pushing and contorting their relationship to fit his own needs. *To fill the void.* Bald fact, he couldn't force true love and family any more than she could force pure joy and happy.

Had he jinxed them a second time by proposing too soon? He'd been so focused on magic, but like Chrissy, what he needed now was the real. This mystery stop at Coyote's agitated his already prickly mood.

Chrissy, on the other hand, vibrated with restrained giddiness. Talk about a curve ball. She shifted in her seat, talking and signing over her shoulder at Mel who was buckled in the backseat, hugging tightly to her stuffed blue dog. "Almost there!"

"And we're going there why?" Mason asked.

"I told you. It's a surprise."

Rolling back his shoulders, he focused on their destination.

The Coyote Club sat at the far end of town, west of Café Caboose and east of Chet's Farm and Feed. Even though the freestanding honky-tonk had been days from going under, Morgan had framed all the windows with colorful twinkling lights and had wrapped the veranda's railing in vining evergreen, giving the club a festive vibe.

Wallowing in misfortune wasn't the former athlete's style. Mason liked that. He liked a lot of things about Bryce Morgan, including his willingness to change and adapt his business for the benefit of his "team". They'd put off in-depth discussions regarding renovation of the club until after the holidays, but Mason was looking forward to their joint venture.

It was another joint venture that had him twisting in the wind.

He glanced over at Chrissy while parking his SUV

alongside Morgan's pickup truck. "Now will you tell me—"

"Nope."

He narrowed his eyes as she hopped out to help Mel out of the backseat. Shook his head when she hurried the kid toward the club's front door.

"Closed for Christmas!" he called, but then the door swung open and Bryce Morgan stepped out, coffee mug in hand.

"I owe you," Chrissy said to the man then hurried Mel inside.

Mason greeted his new partner with a handshake and a wince. "I don't know why Chrissy pulled you away from your family—"

"I do. Don't sweat it, man." The former sports star slapped Mason on the shoulder then retreated into the shadows.

Mason stepped into the club, his eyes adjusting to the dim light and zeroing in on Chrissy and Mel as they shed their coats and made a bee-line toward the dance floor.

Oo-kay.

Curiosity officially off the charts.

Zig-zagging through tables and chairs, Mason frowned at the outdated, inferior speakers flanking the stage. Just one of the things he'd addressed with Morgan when they'd discussed the reinvention of the club.

Clutching her blue dog, Mel gravitated toward the Charlie Brown Christmas tree perched on the corner of the stage.

Mason moved in alongside Chrissy. "What gives?"

"The band playing here this week. Red Riot. They're a quartet of good ol' boys with old school ways. They always leave their axes on stage instead of taking them home. Bryce gave their leader a call and got clearance."

"For?"

She smiled. "Us jamming on their gear. Here," she said, pressing a small packet into his hand. "You're going to need these."

She hurried toward Mel, stooping down and signing to the wide-eyed girl.

Mason looked from the foam earplugs she'd given him, to the stage and Red Riot's set up. He instantly noted the *Stratocaster* and electric fiddle. His heart slammed against his chest. "Oh, hell."

Chrissy dug in her big purse, handing Mel her LED tambourine and then led her up the steps to the three-foot stage.

Mason could scarcely breathe.

He watched as she made use of her own earplugs then turned toward an antiquated rack of sound gear.

"Bryce already powered everything up!" she yelled at Mason. "Brace yourself!"

She pressed a button and music blasted from the speakers. He recognized the progressive rock recording right away. The *Trans-Siberian Orchestra's* instrumental rendition of *Carol of Bells*.

Chrissy cranked the volume even louder.

The room rumbled.

Mel glanced down at her fuzzy pink boots.

She was feeling vibrations through the floor of the stage.

Chrissy swayed to the music, inspiring Mel to do the same then motioned her daughter to shake and hit her tambourine. Then she took up the electric violin and crooked an inviting brow at Mason.

Mouth dry, Mason shed his coat and hopped on stage. He strapped on the beat-up *Strat* and cranked the old *Marshall* amp to ten. He found a pick on top of the amp just as Chrissy put bow to strings.

Mesmerized, Mason watched as the woman he'd first fallen in love with at the Oakley Music and Wine Festival, reconnected with her musical passion.

She played along to the recording, smiling at him, smiling at their daughter.

Mel danced and smacked her tambourine, the LED lights twinkling nearly as much as her big blue eyes.

And Chrissy?

Chrissy sparkled.

A wall of noise pulsed through the air. Mason narrowed his field of listening to her fiddle, his guitar, and Mel's off-beat tambourine.

The perfect blend.

When the song ended, Mason's soul continued to dance.

Along with his daughter.

Tears glistening in her eyes, Chrissy plucked the foam

from her ears and closed the space between her and Mason.

"I believe," she said with a quick glance at Mel, "in our daughter's ability to shine in this world exactly as she is. I believe," she said, pulling the jeweler's box from her hoodie pocket, "in us."

Throat tight with emotion, Mason returned the guitar to the stand and took the ring from the box.

"I want to marry you," she said as he slipped the diamond onto her finger, "because I want to spend my life with you, loving and caring for our daughter. I can't promise I won't have a problem adjusting to your wealth, but I promise not to hold it against you. You're one of the most down-to-earth men I've ever known. I love you, Mason Rivers."

Mason cradled her face and smiled into her eyes. "I love you, Christmas Joy. Happy birthday, baby." He poured his heart into a kiss, his soul singing as she returned his affection in equal measure.

Mel joined in, hugging their legs then bouncing back and thwacking her tambourine.

Mason beamed at his daughter then winked at his future wife. "I think she's requesting another song."

"Making music with my family," Chrissy said with a carefree smile. "Pure joy."

excerpt from

marry poppins

An Impossible Dream Novel

~book three~

Prologue

Once upon a blustery day
Nowhere, Nebraska

Georgina Poppins waffled through life like a leaf caught in the wind. Settling every so often with a man or a job, then being swept back up into the chaos.

At first, she took the constant upheaval in stride. But then she turned thirty-one and more than a little disillusioned. Two of her lifelong friends were engaged to be married. Another owned a successful business. Another juggled three fascinating jobs. Yet another was spiritually attuned and shrouded in a cloud of exhilarating mystery.

Georgie was floundering.

In spite of her dysfunctional upbringing, her deepest desire was to marry a local boy and to start a family of her own. She'd been one of those girls who fantasized about the perfect man, the perfect wedding, the perfect family even before she wore a bra.

Unfortunately, Georgie suffered the same rotten luck with

men as she did with jobs. Her friends had lost count of her defunct relationships and careers.

Georgie hadn't.

Her friends considered her ability to bounce back and adapt—time and again—impressive. They called her multi-talented and resilient.

Mostly she was just desperate enough to try anything once.

Georgie appreciated the positive spin on her inability to shine at any one skill and she did her best to affect a cavalier attitude regarding her string of professional flubs. Teaching assistant, tour guide, party planner, florist, ranch hand, bartender, the shall-not-be-talked-about gig as a lingerie model—to name a few. It's not that she'd bombed at any one of those things. In fact she'd been fairly good at most of those things. But none had been her true calling and all of them had fizzled for some reason or another.

Just like her relationships with men.

Two days after her thirty-first birthday, Georgie hit a wall.

That particular morning, she found out the Nowhere Public Library was closing up shop—forever. That was tragic for a whole lot of reasons, but mostly Georgie hated that it meant one of her best friends was now unemployed. Fortunately, Georgie had been in the position to right Bella's world. Unfortunately, it meant Georgie was now the one scrambling for a job. Again.

Then, only a few hours later while she was stockpiling bargain buys at the grocery, Dirk Banning, a man who'd sworn he was head over heels in love with Georgie, sent her a text—a flipping text—announcing he'd kinda-sorta hooked up with someone else. NO HARD FEELINGS.

Seriously?

She held it together until she reached the privacy of her junker car then—man, oh, man—she indulged in a meltdown of epic proportions. Railing to the universe while strangling her steering wheel and punching her worn leather seats.

"I'm over trying to find my niche! I'm tired of struggling financially!"

And she had lost all hope in ever meeting Mr. Right.

At wit's end, that night Georgie threw caution to the wind. Like her longtime pals, Bella and Chrissy, she contacted

Impossible Dream, an Internet company designed to match people with their most avid desire.

Bella and Chrissy had shot beyond the stars with their farfetched requests and they'd both received prospects from ID.com within a few days.

Mustering optimism, Georgie filled out the required data sheet then stated her Impossible Dream. In a world full of lonely people and single-parent homes, surely it couldn't be that hard to match her with her greatest desire.

Four months later... Georgie was still waiting.

NOTE TO READERS

This series comes from the heart and a longtime love affair with fairy tale romances. I hope I provided you with a bit of joyous escapism! If you enjoyed ENCHANTING CHRISTMAS please consider writing a review on any e-tailer or review site (such as Goodreads). Spreading the word helps me to share the love. Your support is very much appreciated!

Follow the adventures of the Inseparables in the next installment of Impossible Dream—MARRY POPPINS. For a glimpse of something different, visit my website to explore my many worlds. From steampunk to paranormal to contemporary. Something for everyone!

www.bethciotta.com

ACKNOWLEDGMENTS

It takes several professionals to bring a book to life. Special thanks to EJR Digital Art for the fabulous cover art! My appreciation to my critique and editorial team—Elle J Rossi, Cynthia Valero, and Deborah Richardson (DRE&MS). A huge thank you to my marketing advisers: Bards of Badassery. And to Mary Stella for the proof read. You ladies rock! My on-going gratitude to my champion and agent, Amy Moore-Benson. And a heartfelt thank you to my husband, Steve, for supporting my not-so-impossible dream!

Made in the USA
Middletown, DE
19 September 2020